THE ROSE OF DEATH

A KENT DETECTIVE AGENCY MYSTERY

R.P. Hollis
R.P. Hollis Books

Copyright © 2024 by R. P. Hollis

All rights reserved.

No part of this publication may be reproduced, distributed, or transmitted in any form or by any means, including photocopying, recording, or other electronic or mechanical methods, without the prior written permission of the publisher, except as permitted by U.S. copyright law. For permission requests, contact rphollis@rphollisnovels.com

The story, all names, characters, and incidents portrayed in this production are fictitious. No identification with actual persons (living or deceased), buildings, and products is intended or should be inferred. Certain locations and historical events are mentioned but the context in which they are used and the characters who inhabit these pages are purely of my own creation.

Book Cover by 100covers

First edition 2024

TABLE OF CONTENTS

Dedication	V
Preface	VII
1. Old Ghosts Never Die	1
2. It's Always The Innocent Ones	29
3. The Escape	53
4. The Undesirables	77
5. A Frame Job	109
6. The Laughing Flames	137
7. Missing!	163
8. Arrested	191
9. The Luck of the Irish	217
10. An Ambush	241
11. The Sorry Cad	271
12. The Midnight Shift	297
A Word to the Reader	305

Slang from The Rose of Death	307
About the Author	313
Afterword	315
List of Kent Detective Agency Mysteries	317

Dedication

For my mom, who helped me through numerous rewrites.
For my dad, who is hugely supportive.
For my grandparents, who are always there for me.
And for Granddaddy and Grandpa, always.

Preface

This story is set in December 1957-January 1958, and I have included some period words and sayings native to America. There are also some Scottish, Irish, Japanese, and Australian slang words. They may not be familiar, but they are fun. If you're curious about their meaning, you can find the definitions at the end of the story. I also use italics to denote when a character is thinking.

Finally, these books build on each other. They can be read as a standalone, but are so much more fun if you immerse yourself in the world of William Kent.

Chapter One
Old Ghosts Never Die

It was cold outside, although that wasn't surprising so close to the New Year, even in St. Augustine. Many businesses were still closed for Christmas, leaving the office building dark and vacant, with few exceptions. Amid the darkness, a small office on the third floor emanated a warm light, serving as a beacon for those in need. The door proudly proclaimed 'The Kent Detective Agency', although only one man was inside.

His long legs stretched out, the lone occupant of the quiet building was trying to make up for lost sleep. The aching knife wound was only a few months old, and although he had almost recovered from it, he couldn't sleep in his bed. Here, stretched out next to the heater, the cold didn't bother his wound. After yet another sleepless night at home, the detective was dozing contentedly in his chair, thankful for the lack of clients.

That was not how he usually viewed his work; it was his mission to make certain nobody ever felt the abandonment he had endured. As a bonus, working kept the ghosts of his past at bay. Ever since he had started his agency, William Kent had been careful to avoid anything that might remind him of his past, and never accepted a case even remotely tied to his own trauma.

At least that was how it had been when he first started. A lost pet here, maybe a cheating spouse or a missing relative. Nothing too trying. But now, for some inexplicable reason, that had changed. Now it seemed like every case threatened his life; every case was trying to drag him back and leave him forever trapped in the torment of his past. After nearly two years of taxing cases, he was exhausted and battered, physically, mentally, and emotionally. All he wanted was a break.

He would not get it.

Kent suddenly jumped, realizing that he wasn't alone in the room anymore. Somebody was calling him; an unfamiliar voice startling him from his tortured rest. He blinked groggily, hoping to clear his eyes long enough to identify his new companion.

"Excuse me, I am looking for Detective William Kent. I tried knocking, but there was no answer. Do you know where I might find him?"

The detective tensed. The accent was a familiar one, but one that he hadn't heard in over a decade. He wiped the sleep out of his eyes, expecting to find the room empty, and the voice merely an echo from the past. Instead, when his vision finally cleared, he confirmed his visitor was Japanese.

Everything flooded his mind at once—his capture and subsequent torture at the hands of the Imperial Army. The starvation that had driven many of his fellow prisoners to cannibalize the dead and dying. He involuntarily rubbed his arms at the memory, temporarily revealing the bite marks from his fellow prisoners. He had been too weak to stop them, although he wasn't angry at any of them—they were just trying to stay alive. No, he was angry at his captors. They were to blame. Even now, fourteen years later, he remembered every horrifying moment in vivid detail.

"Excuse me, but are you all right?"

His throat was so tight he could barely speak, but he still croaked out a reply. "You were military."

The other man stiffened but refused to back down.

"Hai."

"Not for us, though."

"Hai. I was a soldier in the Imperial Army for Emperor Hirohito. Are you most honorable Detective Kent-san?"

"I am William Kent, but not your friend. There's nothin' for you here," Kent replied roughly.

The man appeared unfazed and continued politely. "I hear many good things about you. They say you most fair man, who help those who need help. And Detective-san, I am in need of help."

Kent clenched his fist as he stood, towering over the other man. Still, the man refused to yield, and stared, unflinching, at the detective. "My most sincere apologies for whatever discomfort my presence has caused you. I assure you I did not take this lightly, and certain things have made my visit necessary. Someone has been threatening me, and I must discover who."

"You came to the wrong place, bud. I try to let the past be, but you best get outta here before I take it out on you."

The smaller man bowed stiffly. "As you wish, Detective-san. I apologize for wasting your time."

With that, he walked out.

As soon as the man was gone, Kent crumpled into a chair and began shaking uncontrollably. Over the last two years, he had faced so many painful demons that he truly believed he had conquered his past. Now he was discovering how utterly wrong he had been. The man's presence picked at scabs Kent assumed had long since healed, and he gripped the chair's arms with white knuckles as he fought for air. He could feel himself getting lightheaded and knew he needed to take a deep breath, but all he could muster were the shallow gasps making him increasingly giddy. A few moments later, he slumped to the floor.

†††††††††††††††††††††††††

Kent blinked slowly, looking up at the ceiling; it was an increasingly familiar view. What had happened? Had somebody attacked him? His chest felt tight, his skin felt like someone had strapped a battery to him, and his arms and legs felt numb. Other than that, and a slight ache in his head from hitting the floor, he felt fine.

Slowly, he sat up and looked for clues. Nothing was out of place, but on the carpet was a leaf that hadn't been there before. It wasn't from anywhere he had been, so it must have come from his visitor. No signs of a struggle. So what had happened?

Pulling himself to his feet, he looked for more evidence. It all came rushing back when he glanced at the door. His visitor wasn't just a prospective client—he had been an enemy. How could someone who had fought against him now be living free and happy in the country he had once worked to destroy? Was there more to the story?

Kent began panicking. Paranoia gripped him as he wondered if his former captors were tracking down survivors to eliminate them. Were they hoping to silence him before he testified to the many Geneva violations he had endured? How far would they go to silence him—was everyone he cared for at risk? He had heard stories about Japanese soldiers so isolated in their bunkers they refused to believe the war had ended. Could this man be one of them?

No matter what the real reason for the man's visit was, Kent knew one thing for certain: he couldn't stay in the office. There he was a sitting duck. For the first time, his central office didn't feel safe. After all, it had already been penetrated once. This second breach had left him thinking about the lack of escape routes. He had planned that—having only one way in meant that if someone came in meaning to harm him, he'd be the one with the advantage. After all, he would hear them coming and have plenty of time to pick them off from behind his oversized walnut desk. But now, that one entrance suddenly didn't feel reassuring; he kept envisioning someone just outside the door, waiting for him to leave his fortress. Kent shuddered.

Get hold of yourself. After all this time, why would anybody care what you have to say? You ain't talked yet, nobody's asked you to, and you think they are worried about you? Besides, he caught you sleeping on the job—he could have offed you then, neat and clean, without givin' you a chance to get ready for him. Instead, he woke you up and asked for your help.

It didn't matter how he tried to explain away the visit, his pulse was still racing. Knowing he'd be of no use to anyone until he calmed down, he tottered unsteadily toward the door. A nice, relaxing drive always calmed him down; maybe it would help him now.

It didn't.

Kent drove around in circles, trying to distract himself with the comfortable familiarity of the historic city. Eventually, he found himself at the city's edge. He couldn't remember the last time he had been there; for all he knew, he never had. If it weren't for his current state of mind, he probably would have never visited this spot. But here he was, and it provided the distraction he needed—he had become so well-acquainted with the historic old city that he assumed he knew all its secrets.

To find out that he didn't was intriguing, and he was studying his surroundings closely.

Something in the distance caught his attention. The biting cold air had nearly everyone seeking the shelter of their homes, and the streets had been empty since he had left his office. He wasn't expecting to see anyone except the occasional straggler, so the movement seized his gaze and demanded an investigation.

Despite the threat of an icy downpour, a crowd had gathered in the distance. It didn't feel right, so he stopped his truck for a better look.

There were eight people in the crowd, forming a circle around their victim, and two of the men had their guns drawn. The figures were clad entirely in white, and he easily recognized their uniforms as belonging to the Ku Klux Klan. This didn't fit their usual tactics, but he wasn't going to wait to find out how far they planned to go. Without hesitation, he shifted the truck into park and started toward them. This wasn't just a brawl; it looked more like an execution.

Suddenly, the crowd separated; a few of the robed figures stepped to the side. Not much, but enough that he could glimpse the man in the center of it all, and he recoiled in disgust as he recognized the victim. The same soldier who had come to him for help hours earlier was now attempting to hold off the white-robed figures alone, but the numbers were overwhelming.

Kent froze, a war waging deep inside his soul as he stood there. Part of him—if he was honest, the biggest part—wanted the man to pay for everything every Allied soldier had suffered, for every American now dead. Each of Kent's brothers-in-arms cried out for vengeance from their graves on the other side of the ocean. It wasn't fair. Those men had families, some of whom would never know for sure what had happened to them, and all of whom had lives to which they would never return. Fathers, sons, husbands, brothers. No matter what their role had been in life, they were all dead now, rotting where they fell or lying in unmarked graves. It almost seemed like poetic justice that he should pay for those crimes now.

Yet there was a small part of him that couldn't stomach the injustice of it. The former Imperial soldier was now injured, but still attempting to defend himself as the two men gleefully fired at his feet.

When one figure pistol-whipped the man, causing him to collapse to the ground, Kent couldn't stand it anymore. It was just so offensive and cowardly that he had to step in.

As one member of the group prepared to fire the kill

shot at the now-unconscious man, Kent fired his own pistol.

The first shot shattered the thug's gun, causing the man to scream in pain as Kent fired again at the other gun-wielding coward. The shot tore through the white hood and neatly creased his head; he fell to the ground in a heap.

Two down, six to go. They turned as one to face the intruder, so Kent kept his M1911 steady. The thought of attacking Americans, no matter who, to protect the life of his enemy turned his stomach. Maybe he wouldn't have to; Kent hoped he could talk them out of whatever they had planned without hurting anyone else.

"Listen, now. I don't know what y'all think you're doing, but you ain't doing anybody any favors with this."

"What do you know about it, pops? Go find a horseshoe championship somewhere. Don't stick your nose where it don't belong, old man."

Kent bristled, his knuckles white from gripping the gun so tightly. Still, he refused to give up on a peaceful approach just because his adversaries were rude. "Look, he's already down. One of you should've been able to put him down easy; there's no need for all this."

"Why are you sticking your neck out for a Jap,

anyway? You must've been one of those draft dodgers or you wouldn't even think about it."

Kent's face turned an unholy shade of red as he stood to his full height, towering over the mob, but he still refused to acknowledge his rage. "All I'm saying is, you're the ones taking the coward's way out. Eight-to-one ain't exactly fair odds. And if that wasn't enough, two of you have pistols and one has a blackjack. You really that afraid of a little Jap?"

"Like he deserves better."

"No matter what he was, he's American now. If he committed a crime, turn him in to the cops. If he didn't, you got your free punch and then some for whatever he and his kind did to your kin."

One of the young men sneered. "He's no American. You and me, we're American. He's no better than the coloreds. Hitler almost had it right, and if he hadn't tied in with them, he'd have won easily."

"Kid, I tried talkin', but you ain't got enough sense to talk back. Some of the best men I served with were colored. And they were worth more than the whole gang of you put together. We all fought together so everybody would have rights, and that includes your right to be stupid and his right to breathe. Now, you either back off or get ready for a long-overdue whoopin'."

Three of the men moved toward him, while the other three stayed by the two figures on the ground.

As one drew back his leg to kick the prone Japanese man, the Imperial grabbed it and deftly twisted, sending the man to the ground. The middle-aged man then rolled out of the way of the other two, wiping the blood from his eyes just in time to allow another to strike.

On the other side of the drive, Kent was still trying to avoid shooting anyone else. He used the butt of his pistol to drop one as another raced headfirst into his gut, knocking the breath out of his chest and allowing the third to join the fray.

With Kent doubled over wheezing, the second delinquent landed a kidney punch. Kent winced but managed a throat punch that incapacitated the man before grabbing the head of the last man standing and slinging him across the gravel into the figure currently kicking the injured man. Quickly, he hurried to scoop up his unlikely ally, then peeled off.

Kent shook his head in disbelief as he glanced in his rearview. "Can't believe I just did that, and to save you."

The former soldier moaned, and Kent glanced over at him. "Reckon I can stand giving you one more favor before I get you out of my life for good. I'll drop you off at the hospital pronto."

"Thank you, Detective-san, no. I cannot go there."

Something in the man's tone resonated with Kent. There were only three things the detective feared: spiders, hospitals, and his captors. Despite having thought moments before that they had nothing in common, Kent realized with a jolt that he had just found their first common ground.

Still, that wasn't enough to make them friends. "Look, bub. I get not wantin' to be a pincushion—if there's anybody who knows what a healthy fear of rubbing alcohol and candy stripers can do to your head, it's me. But I ain't goin' to do anything more than that for ya, so don't think we're gonna sit around drinkin' beer together singin' kumbaya. I don't owe you any more than what I've already given you, and plenty would say I've gone soft and given you too much already. So, like I said, I'm dumpin' you out the first chance I get."

"Please, Detective-san. If they find me, they hurt my family. It is why I come to you in first place. I must...keep them...safe."

When his passenger suddenly became quiet, Kent glanced over and saw the man had blacked out and was now slumped over against the window. *Well, that's just not fair. Now what?*

As much as he hated himself for it, he knew the man must have been desperate to take care of his family. No matter how much Kent wanted to be done with the man, he couldn't leave a family unprotected. No, it didn't matter that he thought his companion deserved it. He wasn't going to let innocent civilians suffer.

His next problem was where to take the man. He wasn't about to drag any of his own family into this mess—not his right-hand man, Jimmy O'Sullivan, who had been shot while rescuing him, and certainly not Jimmy's wife Doris. She had served as a wartime nurse and seen firsthand the horrors the Axis was capable of. And once the war was over, she helped them both put their lives back together. It was she who Kent always turned to if he had a medical emergency.

He would not ask either of them to relive it, and he certainly would not endanger his family for an enemy.

No, he would handle this alone.

Thankfully, his house was, for the moment, empty. That was a blessing: Chad Campbell, his roommate, had been in the same prison camp as Kent, and his brother was killed in the escape. It had taken time, but the two had become friends—and he was the only person on the planet who hated the Imperial Army more than William Kent.

Thankfully, he was on a walkabout, so Kent felt safe enough to take the man home until he figured out a more suitable arrangement.

†††††††††††††††††††††††††††

SEVERAL HOURS LATER, KENT had patched the man up and had him on a pallet in the laundry room. The injured man still hadn't come to, and Kent was beginning to think he had made a mistake by skipping the hospital.

Before he could decide what to do next, he heard a knock at the front door. A quick glance through the peephole confirmed his pistol wasn't necessary; it was only his friend, Lauren LaRue.

With a sigh of relief, he opened the door. "What's up, Lars?"

The young woman pushed past him, studying him as he closed the door. "I went to work this afternoon and found the office empty. You didn't leave a note, William, and we had an agreement. If you decide to work something dangerous, you are supposed to have backup."

"It wasn't anything dangerous."

"And I suppose you have some oceanfront property in Arizona. I do not believe that for a moment—your hand looks as though it is broken, and you're groaning every time you take a deep breath. So, what happened?"

Kent hated lying but was determined not to involve her in whatever mess he had just waded into, and was a little embarrassed at the thought of someone finding out who was in his house. "I slammed my hand in the freezer, and it's so cold that cut's started hurting again. You know, the one where somebody tried to gut me? It's been actin' up somethin' fierce, what with this blasted chill in the air."

Lauren eyed him suspiciously but didn't push him any farther. She knew from experience she wasn't going to get anything else out of him until he was ready. "Fine. You are a grown man, after all. I have to get home now; Luke and I have a date in an hour and he will not be pleased if I am late because I was checking up on you."

Kent grinned despite himself. Ever since young Luke had mistaken him for Lauren's father, the two hadn't gotten along well, mainly because the young man was still embarrassed about what had happened. It didn't help that Kent had threatened the youth with bodily harm if he ever hurt Lauren, either.

The disadvantage was Luke had been so terrified that he kept trying to convince Lauren she needed to distance herself from Kent. That hadn't happened, and the two men had come to an uneasy truce. As long as Kent stayed out of their relationship, Luke would do the same. But since Lauren had followed Kent and the O'Sullivans to Virginia and helped solve 'The Fatal Reunion', Luke had become increasingly clingy.

It was understandable, given the circumstances, but it was taking a toll on Lauren. Besides, the youth was clumsy to the point of being dangerous, and although Kent wanted Lauren to have all the normal fun that twenty-three-year-olds have, he was sure that the relationship was fizzling out. Either way, as long as Luke didn't hurt her, Kent was determined to keep his end of the deal and stay out of it.

Besides, Kent now had the perfect excuse to get rid of her before she discovered his secret. "It's best not to keep your beau waitin'."

Lauren huffed as she began to leave.

A sudden crash stopped her, but Kent blocked her from investigating. "That blasted cat keeps findin' its way in. I gotta seal up that panel to the water heater better, so it can't get in anymore. See ya, Lars."

Once again, she shook her head. He held his breath; she had the makings of a fine detective, but he was crossing his fingers, hoping she would accept his explanation.

It wasn't so unlikely; the cat left its muddy paw prints on her car every time Lauren visited and had snuck past her more than once. Hopefully, that would be enough to convince her.

Lauren hesitated. It seemed plausible, and she had no reason to doubt him—aside from his tone. She had known Kent long enough to recognize when he was being less than truthful, but he clearly didn't want her there. And he was right about her date; she was looking forward to 'Legend of the Lost'. It was her turn to choose the movie, and who didn't like John Wayne? It would certainly be more fun than arguing with Kent. So, after reminding him not to do anything without backup, she chose to leave for her date.

Finally, Kent was alone again. He hurried to the laundry room to check on his unwelcome guest, finding him leaning on the ironing board. "All right, bud, spill. Why'd I bring you here instead of letting you be somebody else's problem? What makes you think those knuckleheads would go after your family?"

"I do not wish to be burden, Detective-san. If you would be so kind as to take me home, I will leave you to your work. I am very sorry for troubling you."

"In for a penny, in for a pound. You got my ribs all busted up and made me lie to my friend. After all your kind did to me, the least you can do is give me some answers."

"Detective-san, I apologize for the trouble, but will bother you no further."

"You came to me."

"And I see my error. The past cannot be forgotten so quickly. Perhaps it will be in the lifetime of my children, but not in ours. We who lived it cannot forget."

"Now see here, if I can get past it—"

"Because only you Americans suffered in the war. I am in your debt for what you did, but will indebt myself to you no further. Please, Detective-san, let us not argue over that which we cannot change."

Kent wasn't giving up so easily. After so much time had passed, he finally had someone physical to blame. "All right, bub. Just what exactly do you think you suffered? Your people started this. We didn't want war, but your pals went and bombed the Arizona. We never woulda got dragged into that mess if we woulda just been left alone."

"Perhaps, perhaps not. But your people were not completely blameless."

"Oh, and yours were? You people fight dirty. Those hell ships didn't get named that for bein' beacons of hope."

"Hai. Those are stain on our history. True, much wrong was done. But can you truthfully say all blame was ours?

"I came home injured. I still wish to serve my emperor and bring honor to my family, despite the stories of those 'hell ships', as you call them. We hear stories about them and the treatment the prisoners received. There was no honor there, but I heard stories about what you Americans do as well.

"Regretfully, my injuries were such that I could not return to the service. My wife come to meet me, and we were to return to Hiroshima. It was the ancestral home of my family, and it is where they lived still. All of them—my parents, my brothers, my sisters, my cousins, my aunts, and my uncles. It was only good fortune that we were not there already when they dropped the first bomb.

"My Tsuma and I try to return. We hope that someone survive, but only one was my cousin. She tell us everyone else dead, and after two days of suffering, she too died. Tsuma was concerned that another bomb would be dropped on us, but I dismissed her until the second one was dropped the next day. Then I decided, no matter my personal feelings, to go to the one place Americans would never bomb. Only after my arrival did I learn what your country did to its own citizens because they looked like me, not you."

Kent tensed. His efforts to claw back some peace were backfiring spectacularly, and he was so angry that he tasted blood. He started when he realized it wasn't just a bad memory—he had bitten through his lip.

Feeling like he had to speak for those who couldn't, Kent pressed on. Tired of searching for words that wouldn't come, he did something he had never considered doing in his life.

Enraged, he threw aside his jacket and tore off his shirt, revealing the scars he worked so hard to conceal. "I can't thank your kind for all of these, but a good many of them came from the hospitality of your 'honorable' people."

He began pointing to each scar as he named them. "These came from your guards when they'd whip me until they tore the skin off my back. These on my arms are from those your friends left to starve, who got so hungry they thought I was the biggest turkey they'd ever seen and tried to eat me whole. And these burns came from one of those hell ships, unmarked as transport, and sank as an enemy combatant. My soldiers had no way of knowing we were on that ship, and you Japs left them locked below to burn alive. I tried to get some of them clear, but no such luck and the oil burned me as thanks.

"So you'll have to excuse me if my heart ain't broken because we used your own tactics against you. Y'all started targeting civilians long before we did. If ya don't believe me, ask any Tommy Atkins that survived the blitz, or any of the orphans that survived by spending weeks hiding in the dark."

The Japanese man clutched the board to steady himself, dizzy and on the verge of blacking out again. "So, now we are equally suspicious of each other. I have burdened you enough. If you would be so kind as to take me to my home, we shall return to our lives."

The detective begrudgingly began helping him to the truck. "Look, I didn't do any of this 'cause of you. You said your family needed help. I might not care one way or the other about you, but nobody can ever say I abandoned a family. So spill already."

Kent waited for an answer. After several moments, he realized he was bearing the full weight of his companion; the man was unconscious again.

He was ashamed to have ever allowed the man in his house, but still felt obligated to keep him alive. Looking at his former enemy, he wondered how many of his friends the man had killed.

There was no sound in the house except the breathing of the two men. A sudden ringing shattered the silence and dragged Kent back to the present. He put the man back on his makeshift pallet, then hurried to answer his phone.

He mopped the sweat off his forehead as he answered, gulping nervously and hoping he didn't sound as guilty as he felt. "Hello?"

The voice of his best friend came from the other end of the line. "Hiya, Boss. I was planning to take the kids up to Georgia. I heard it snowed, and me rugrats enjoyed it so much when it snowed last year, mo ghrá and I thought we'd surprise them with a quick snowball fight."

"Sorry I can't tag along! Y'all have fun."

"Are ye all right, Boss? Sure and ye sound a bit off."

Kent swallowed, clenching his fist as he tried to steady his voice. "I'm fine, Jimmy. Just got a ton of paperwork, and a cheatin' husband to spy on until he messes up. Y'all go on now, enjoy yourselves."

"Are ye certain sure? Ye do not sound good at all."

"Just a long day leading to a long night, and on top of everything, I'm comin' down with somethin'. Don't worry about me none."

"Well, if ye say so," Jimmy's voice was still full of

doubt. "If ye need me, though, leave a message with ma. She's staying put. Something about it being cold enough here without going to find some frozen water. We'll be calling her sometimes to let the kids tell her about everything, so she can pass along any message ye may have for me. Take care, Boss."

Kent heard the pleading tone in his friend's voice. He felt bad for lying to him, but not bad enough to change his mind. "I will. I'll see ya when I see ya."

With that, Kent slammed down the receiver, checked on his houseguest, and went to his room.

It didn't take long for the detective to decide that sleep was futile. Instead, he stood guard over his visitor. Kent didn't know who he was watching out for—the men who had attacked his 'guest', or the man himself. Whoever it might be, he would be ready.

Night came and went. The detective had stayed at his post since sundown, and kept a healthy distance between them, going near the man only to doctor on him. Now, it seemed the man was finally coming around.

"How ya feelin', fella?"

"I will live. Why...?"

"I brought you home yesterday after a welcomin' committee set you up. Ya ain't half bad as a fighter, I'll say that much for you. And if you're askin' why you're still here, I got three good answers for ya. First and foremost, you weren't in any condition to go anywhere. Second, you never told me where you live, so I couldn't take you home if I wanted to. And last, you said your family is in trouble. So, I'm willing to call a truce, least 'til we get everything straightened out."

"Thank you, Detective-san, but I must go home now, and that is my final favor I must ask. I will deal with this matter myself."

"Not to put a damper on anythin', but I'd say this is a little bigger than you. You admitted ya needed help before. If your family is in trouble, ya really oughta get your head outta your rear. I'm offerin' you an olive branch, and you'd do well to take it. Old ghosts never die, and that's a fact, but I ain't anglin' for us to be friends. Goin' after family is a no-go. The quicker I solve this for you, the quicker we get out of each other's lives. You came for help, and sucker I am, I plan to give it to you. Let's start small. You know my name; I'm William Kent, and you are?"

"Forgive me, Detective-san. I am Masao Nagasaki. I am honored by your offer. However—"

"Look, pal, I don't like you. But I ain't leavin' your family in the lurch. Spit it out already."

"As you wish. My community is being targeted by the violent criminals you met. Workplaces have been destroyed, homes burned, entire families disappear in the dead of night. This has ruined many lives."

"What do the cops say?"

"Most of my neighbors were in the camps. They do not trust police any more than you trust me. I do not blame them. It is most difficult to admit you are not strong enough to keep your family safe and ask your enemy for help."

He paused and stared pointedly at Kent, who returned the glare. After a few minutes spent studying each other, Masao continued. "I admit, I wanted to keep our problems within our borders. But then my little girl come home with a white rose, and it was too much. I did not want her to be next, so I ask questions. But there were few left to ask, and nobody who remain had answers. So, I come to you."

Kent was skeptical. "Because of a flower?"

"In my culture, the white rose can symbolize things such as purity, but also death. What is more innocent than a child? They threaten my daughter, and I will not let my family be tormented. Although most difficult, I put aside my past to bring them here for safety. I am not afraid for myself, mind you. I am a soldier and have faced death before. But I do not know where to look, and I would stand out looking for them where they live. I need somebody who look like them to discover their true intent."

Kent chuckled despite himself. "If you want somebody to blend in, ya might have come to the wrong place. I don't think I've ever blended in anywhere in my life, but I make do. I am good at gettin' to the bottom of a mess, and I can't stand bullies. If you stay outta my way, I'll figure it out for ya.

"Now, you seem pretty okay to me, and I'm sure your wife is worried sick about you. She's probably just as qualified to fix you up as I am, maybe more so, so if ya just point me in the right direction, I'll take you home."

"Dōmo arigatōgozaimashita, Detective-san. I am sorry for the trouble, but—"

"Yeah, I know. Let's get you home now, an' worry 'bout the rest later."

Chapter Two
It's Always The Innocent Ones

Masao struggled down the stairs to Kent's truck, accepting help only if he had no choice, while Kent watched him and offered assistance as little as possible.

The ten-minute drive to the man's house was equally silent. Masao struggled to stay upright and conscious, while Kent tried to ensure they didn't have a tail and that nobody saw the two of them together.

When they got to the place Masao called home, Kent realized the man was increasingly unsteady. Reluctantly, he helped the unsteady man cover the uneven ground until they reached the front door. He knocked loudly as Masao called to his wife, but the house remained silent.

Kent found the spare key exactly where Masao said it would be and opened the door.

After hearing his new client's description of what had been happening, the detective was prepared for a bloodbath. Not wanting the man to slow him down or find his family dead, he sat Masao on a bench outside and worked quickly to clear the house. In each new room, he expected an ambush or a body.

Instead, there was nothing. No broken furniture, no shattered china, just a well-kept house.

Despite his frustration at being left out of his own house, Masao knew he would be no help in his current condition. If somebody had his family, he wanted them dealt with instantly. For a moment, he debated staying outside and out of Kent's way, but he decided no one would be as motivated to protect his loved ones as he was. Struggling, he followed Kent inside.

The house was small, so it took Kent only a few minutes to search it, and he was finished by the time Masao reached the front door. He found a note written in Japanese, but he only knew a few written words; nothing on the paper looked familiar. So, as soon as Masao was safely seated on the couch, he handed him the note and waited impatiently for the translation.

Masao studied it before staring blankly at the wall. After several moments, Kent decided he had given his client enough time and cleared his throat.

"What? Oh, I am sorry. This say my wife has been looking for me since past midnight, and that she plans to check here every two hours to see if I have returned. If my calculation correct, I think she should be here in twenty minutes. Thank you, I shall be all right now. You may leave and hopefully uncover who behind the threat to my family. The sooner you can accomplish this, the sooner you and I return to our lives and put this regrettable ordeal behind us."

It was a strange feeling the two men shared. Once sworn enemies, they now found themselves in the awkward position of working together. Yet as much as Kent longed to follow his client's instructions, leaving the injured man alone in his condition was impossible. That left them no choice but to share the room until the return of the Nagasaki family.

Luckily for Masao Nagasaki, he was still too woozy to feel the oppressive uneasiness that pulsed through the room.

Unluckily for Kent, he wasn't. His new client kept talking about his family; focusing on them gave him a reason to fight. Meanwhile, Kent was doing everything in his power to force his own family from his mind, and Masao was making that difficult. The man's condition might have forced the hapless detective to stay, but the last thing he wanted was to think about what his family would say about his current case. And despite the sympathy he felt for his client's dilemma, Kent still did not like him.

The minutes ticked by loudly, thanks to the stately old grandfather clock. Neither man spoke again, and each became so enthralled by the silence that they both jumped when a new sound broke through the room.

Kent hoped the slamming door meant the family had returned, but still prepared for a fight. Although it took only a few moments for the unseen person to wiggle a key in the lock, he had already concealed himself in the corner, his M1911 in his hand and ready for combat.

When the figure stepped out of the blinding sunlight, Kent immediately holstered his weapon. The tiny woman who walked in was certainly not a threat to him, and he recognized her from a photograph on the end table as the missing wife.

Not wanting to startle her, he waited until she had reached her husband before making his presence known.

The woman jumped, but her husband quickly clasped her hand reassuringly. "Misa, this most honorable detective William Kent, who will help us."

"If he help us, why you gone so long? What happen?

You hurt?" The woman fired her questions at her husband accusingly, but her suspicious gaze was fixated on Kent.

After that, the couple began speaking in Japanese. Kent understood enough to know that he was intruding, and some of her words made him blush. With nothing else to do inside, he bolted outdoors, pulling the door firmly behind him.

Despite the frigid weather, he was sweating so profusely he couldn't see. After wiping his eyes, he blinked in surprise. Standing in front of him was a little girl in a smocked nightgown, holding her teddy bear by one arm and studying him intently.

"Hi there, cutie. What's your name?"

She looked him over one last time before nodding, apparently satisfied with what she saw. Stepping toward him, she held out her hand. "My name is Suki."

Kent kissed the offered hand, and she smirked. *Little girls love princesses, if Rita is to be believed. Well, that and beating up their brothers.* Aloud, he commented, "I knew a little girl named Sachiko once."

Her eyes grew wide, and she stepped closer to him, ignoring the orders of her older brothers. "You pwetty smart. Is you going to laugh at me now?"

"No, Suki, I think you've got a beautiful name. Is this

your house?"

"Nah-uh."

"Well, whose is it?"

"My daddy, siwwy."

It took all his strength not to burst out laughing at her serious delivery, but he didn't want to hurt her feelings. Before he could answer, Misa Nagasaki called her children inside. The boys marched along obediently, giving Suki and the detective both a wide berth.

Suki answered the silent rebuke with a retort of her own by sticking her tongue out at them before trying to scramble up Kent's leg. Once again armed with his experience with his niece, he grinned before reaching down and balancing her on his back. Despite the pain in his chest, he gave his best impression of a gallop and was rewarded with a happy squeal.

The couple had very different reactions to his entrance. Despite his efforts to remain impassive, Masao's eyes twinkled with pride, while Misa's face bore an intense scowl, clearly meant to subdue her daughter. When that failed, she redirected her withering gaze to Kent, who met it without flinching.

Although unmoved by the rebuke, Kent wanted to respect the mother's feelings, and gently set Suki down and nudged her toward her parents.

The little girl was having none of it; she clung defiantly to her new friend. Kent tried—and failed—to edge her closer to her mother, but he was secretly thankful for the diversion. It kept his hands busy and gave him something to think about besides his strange predicament.

When she scurried into his lap and began bouncing herself on his knee, he finally took the hint and gave up. Avoiding the daggers from Misa Nagasaki's eyes, he played 'Ride a Cock Horse to Banbury Cross' with the delighted little girl.

"Ma'am, have you got any ideas who might have sent the flower?"

Misa spoke in a clipped tone. "I take care of it myself if I could. This our business, not for outsiders. Concern only family. If Masao would—"

Her husband silenced her with a withering glance of his own, and she clenched her jaw as he replied. "Life never easy here, but nothing like this. Young ones have no respect."

"When did this first start?"

Misa's stony silence prompted Masao to answer again. "We were not bothered until two months ago, but then we began receiving threats. The windows in our car were all shattered, then our mailbox smashed. It was regrettable, but not enough to change our lives. Only more recently has it become such that I was forced to seek your aid. My Misa, as you can see, is not pleased with my decision. She believes I should do what they say and sell our lives. This has not been easy for her."

Despite having used Suki successfully to avoid looking at Misa, Kent discreetly glanced at the angry mother when he asked if she had anything to add.

As soon as he saw her, he regretted it. The look of contempt on her face left a tight feeling in his chest that choked him, and for a moment, he felt guilty. Her life had been difficult through no fault of her own. Masao, sure. He shouldn't have ever fought against America. As far as Kent was concerned, he was paying his dues now. But nobody else had done anything wrong, and little Suki reminded Kent too much of Rita O'Sullivan for him to allow anything to happen to her. If he felt that way after only a few minutes with the kid, he could only imagine how her mother felt.

Masao had been carefully watching his daughter, and now he motioned for her to join him. Only then did Suki finally relinquish her place on Kent's knee, happily skipping to her father and grabbing his neck. The injured man allowed her to snuggle there with him for a few moments before sending her to her brothers in the other room.

With Suki's departure, all warmth left the room, replaced by the icy silence of the angry Misa and dazed Masao.

After several awkward moments, Kent cleared his throat. "I'm gonna head out now and get to work unless there's somethin' else you wanna tell me."

Masao and Misa agreed he knew everything now. Eager to escape, the detective didn't press it any farther. There was nothing he wanted more than to flee the angry woman, so he eagerly pulled himself out of the chair.

As he struggled to his feet, he made a mental note to never sit on anything so close to the ground ever again. It was costing him precious seconds, and he couldn't wait to get in his truck and drive far away, fast.

Although he had planned to go back to the office, he drove right past it. The thought of going back to work on the case so soon left his stomach churning. He couldn't face his friends—not even their shadows in the place where they worked together. The war had taken enough. Just because he had been dragged back into the past didn't mean that he would let his friends be pulled back with him. He could already feel it gnawing at him, and he needed quiet. Time to think. He wouldn't get that at work, where anyone could drop in at any moment, so he kept driving.

†††††††††††††††††††††††††

THE SUN WAS SETTING when a car pulled alongside a baby blue '56 Chevy truck. The man inside frowned; finding it by the swamp wasn't a good sign. It wasn't easy for him to get out, but he did it as quickly as he could before leaning on the crutches and limping purposefully into the marsh.

He didn't have to go far to find the truck's owner. Oblivious to the freezing temperature, William Kent was absently staring at the water, skipping stones. Thoroughly lost in his own thoughts, the detective didn't hear the second man approaching, or even notice him sit down.

After several silent skips punctuated by the ripple of each stone, the second man picked up a stone and gave it a halfhearted throw.

Another skip, another disgusted grunt. After several more, the detective began ignoring his companion again. Finally, the second man spoke.

"Never had much time for such as a lad, but sure and it seems simple enough. Still, I think I be getting better with each throw. Do ye care for a little bet?"

Silence.

"Sure and we could have something simple. 'Twould need to be interesting, though, or what would be the point of it all?

"I have it. If ye win, I'll trade my crutches for a mop and Doris' apron for a day while me rugrats ride on me back. But if ye lose, ye paint the Indian pink."

A deep chuckle escaped Kent despite his foul mood. "Jimmy, you might be able to do a lot of things, but I've got ya beat here. Maybe you oughta think this through before making that bet."

Jimmy was relieved to see the faintest glimmer in Kent's eyes and was determined to lure his friend into a better frame of mind. "Are ye afraid to bet me, Boss?"

"I've known you the better part of two decades, Jimmy. And never once have you ever picked up a skipping stone."

"Maybe, but I have already made me peace with me bet. What do ye say?"

"All right, but no bellyaching when I snap a few pictures for posterity."

Jimmy smiled patiently. "Well, ye may get a chance, Boss, but surely ye do not mind giving me a few throws to warm up?"

"Makes no difference to me. Go ahead, I'd hate to take

any more advantage of you than I already am."

Jimmy took his practice shots, each one slightly farther than the last, and Kent tugged his collar nervously. He hadn't had the motorcycle long—only around a year. It was a project when he bought it, a gift intended to cheer Lauren up by reminding her of happier times. He had worked hard to get it running again, but he had wrecked it soon after he finally had it drivable. Since then, he had invested a lot of blood and sweat to fix it, and painting it pink was the worst thing he could think of.

Still, none of the throws went as far as his. Hoping that would be enough to win, he skipped another rock. It went far past any of the others and was a personal best, and Kent exhaled with relief. For a fleeting second, he thought he had won—until Jimmy took his shot.

Jimmy's throw was beautiful. With a twist of his wrist, Jimmy sent the pebble at a perfect arc, and it easily sailed past where Kent's rock had landed.

Kent stuttered, his mouth agape. "B-but, you never?"

Jimmy grinned at his friend's horrified expression. "No, I never—at least not until I had me kids. Sure and ye remember them, right, boyo? And ye have noticed me little cailín óg loves to throw things? Do ye really think I just let her throw what she can get her hands on? Or do ye think I learned how to do this so I could teach them to throw something that would be hurting nothing? I may have missed most of their lives, but I've had the chance to fix that. And if ye ever need a marble shooter—or someone to play jacks or pickup sticks—I be your man."

Kent stared at the last ripple, dumbfounded.

After a few moments, Jimmy decided his friend had suffered enough and burst out laughing. "Boss, I'll not be marching off the winner. I hustled ye. But we do need to get ye out of this wind before ye catch your death of cold."

Kent grinned in relief as he stood, his joints popping in disapproval after sitting still for so long. After taking a moment to stretch, he lifted Jimmy to his feet, and the friends headed to their vehicles.

Kent's foul mood was impossible to ignore, and it wasn't long before Jimmy decided his friend needed some help if he was going to get back to his normal chipper self. After all, 'sharing' was not something William Kent did. "Boss, what ails ye? Ye missed work all day, did not call anyone, and Lauren said ye were actin' strange. So, what is it?"

"Nothin' I want to talk about."

Kent stood there, his hand on the truck, before finally speaking again. "I took a case I shouldn't have. I can't believe I did, but I took it. And because I can't say no, I'm lettin' everybody down."

"Well, Boss, what makes this case so bad?"

"Who the client is."

"Would this case bother ye if somebody else asked ye to do it? Are ye doing something ye ought not?"

"No, I wouldn't think twice if somebody else had asked me."

"What happens if ye do not do it?"

How did Jimmy always manage to simplify things so well? Kent sighed. "An innocent kid gets hurt, maybe worse."

"Then ye have no choice. If ye would do it for anyone else, and it's nothing ye would not do for anyone else, ye must help. Ye aren't doing it for your client, ye be doing it for his family. Ye have naught to feel guilty for, so why do ye look so ashamed? Take it easy on yourself, boyo, before you worry yourself back into the hospital."

Kent nodded slowly.

"I mean it, Boss. I trust ye, and ye have the strongest conscience of anyone I know. Ease up, Boss. Ye are doing right."

Jimmy meant well, but his reassurances only made Kent feel even guiltier. He was sure he'd lose his brother if he told Jimmy the truth. Jimmy was on crutches because of the Japanese; he had lost ten years of his life to the wounds he had suffered. And what about Doris? She would be just as hurt. Lauren was too young to remember much about the war, so maybe she'd forgive him, but nobody else would understand.

Yet as much as he hated to admit it, Jimmy was right. Now that he had met little Suki, he would not leave her to the tender mercies of some Nazi wannabes. *It's always the innocent ones that suffer.* "You're right. Reckon I oughta get to work so I can close this case pronto, though. Just remember you told me to take this case if anything happens."

"Boss, 'tis late. Ye should head home, then start up again first thing in the morning."

After several minutes, Jimmy won the debate, and the two parted ways.

When Kent got home, the moon was high in the sky and bathed the truck in its brilliant glow. He had successfully dragged out his trip home, but now he was out of excuses. No more delaying; he had promised to relax. Relax. How? His skin was crawling. There was no way he could go to sleep, so he put on his new Ella Fitzgerald record, tossed his hat neatly onto its peg, then collapsed into his custom-made wing chair and allowed the music to wash over him.

An hour passed. Kent had dozed off, but something had startled him. The record had stopped, and he was alone. Still, he was sure that he had heard something. Or had he only dreamed it?

Suddenly, Kent heard it again, and this time he recognized it. Someone was tapping at his door. One hand clutched his M1911, while the other reached for the door.

He blinked in surprise when he saw who was there. "Mrs. Nagasaki, what brings you here? I got the feelin' you wanted no part of this."

"Can I come inside? Prying eyes never learn truth before spreading lies."

"Oh, yes ma'am. I wasn't thinking. Come on in,"

Misa stepped past him haughtily and marched inside before sitting primly in Kent's chair, forcing him to sit in one of the shorter chairs he kept for his visitors. "I come for one thing only. Drop husband's case, I pay you for your time."

"Now, ma'am, I understand why you might be hesitatin' to keep me on, but I aim to give it everything I've got, same as any other case."

"I only have problem if you stay. If you stop, husband let us return home. Everything fine. Even if you stop these people, what good it do me? Someone else come, finish what they start. I take my family home, not stay in this place. I tired of my children being threatened because they not like everybody else. You give husband false hope. He think, you catch bad guys, everything all right. We live happy ever after. I know better, you do too. My babies always in danger here. You tell Masao no help, he give up. Then we go home. You get less Japanese, I get less Americans. Everybody happy. You keep working, we stay, somebody get caught, you get paid, leave, somebody finish job, kill us. You maybe happy, us not so much. Tell him no."

Kent shook his head in disbelief. He had just been handed a get-out-of-jail-free card, the perfect excuse to drop a case he hated to have. He couldn't believe what he was about to say. "I'm sorry, ma'am, but I promised your husband. I don't want any part of this either, but I ain't just going to leave you twisting in the wind. And even after I catch them, if somebody else threatens you, just call me and I'll come back. These people are just getting started. They began with mailboxes, moved on to windows, then threats, and now they've beaten your husband. They ain't going to quit just because you asked nicely."

"We sell house, then go. No ask."

"So, you put up a for sale sign, and they just sit back

and wait for you to leave? Somehow I don't see that happenin'."

"There are people who want my house. I sell, we leave, everybody win."

"Ma'am, this is somethin' you oughta talk over with your husband. Until he tells me the house is sold and it's time for me to quit, I plan to keep workin', just to be on the safe side. Think of me as your backup plan."

Misa stood carefully, her gloved hands touching only each other, as though she would get contaminated by touching anything. Once again, she pushed past him. Before he could wriggle out of his seat, she opened the door and stormed out.

Kent watched incredulously as she left. Didn't she know how hard this was for him? He was helping her, and she was acting like he was the one threatening her family. She hadn't even bothered to close the door behind her, so the baffled detective pushed it shut, twisting the knob to make certain it clicked. Something gooey stuck to his hand, so he wiped it off before settling back into his chair. It didn't take long before he started nodding off, the weight of the world crushing his chest.

Thirty minutes later, Kent woke up, his stomach rolling. His clothes were drenched with sweat, his body shaking; another ghost from his past was back, demanding an explanation for his treachery. He tried to breathe, calm himself, to do anything to get rid of the pressure that was suffocating him. Nothing was working. He was getting shakier by the second, and his stomach was still turning, so he started toward the bathroom.

A loud crash stopped him. Had he knocked something over? He didn't think so, but couldn't be sure. If only he could think! There wasn't time, though. He heard another crash, and it definitely came from outside. That meant he had company, and it probably wasn't the neighbor's cat. There was no time to shake off whatever funk was tormenting him; he needed to check it out.

Still groggy, he stumbled out the door to investigate. He barely had time to step outside when somebody pushed him down the stairs. Before Kent could react, he was tumbling down, unable to protect himself. Trying to stop the fall was pointless; he barely understood what was happening. There was no way he could do anything to help himself, so he thudded and thumped until he lay in a bruised heap at the bottom of the staircase.

The night wasn't finished with the weary detective

yet. He had barely lifted his head when he felt a searing pain in his chest, then another.

The pain sliced through his confusion and temporarily jolted him back to the present, and he glanced up to see what was happening. There, standing to his right. A shadow—was it his imagination? It was hard to see through the bloody haze. There it was again—and another, and another. Six white-clad silhouettes, almost impossible for him to distinguish from the moonlight. They had circled him, just as they had Masao the day before, and a gleeful chuckle accompanied each vicious kick.

Dazed though he was, Kent knew he had to act fast if he wanted to see his niece and nephew grow up. Despite his shaking hand fumbling as he searched for the P38 can opener he always wore around his neck, he finally clasped it and yanked it loose.

Another leg closed in on his face. This time, he was ready; he lashed out with the can opener and sliced the flesh, causing the man to retreat with a yelp. Several more attempts were met with the same result, and several pained howls pierced the night's silence. Lights began switching on up and down the beachfront, and the mob limped away, cursing softly, leaving Kent lying on the ground.

After several minutes, Kent managed to drag himself to the steps and sit up. Waving to his neighbor across the street, he tried to gather his wits. Everything was hurting, especially his stomach. It hurt worse than ever.

Finally, he gave up. If the world wouldn't stop spinning for him, he'd just push through until he could find his bed. It wasn't the first time this had happened, although it seemed to be a little harder to fight each time. Still, it was probably nothing a good night's sleep couldn't cure, and Kent was so groggy there was no doubt in his mind that he'd pass out as soon as he got into bed.

Reassuring himself that this was nothing new, Kent pulled himself up the stairs, one agonizing step at a time. A quick stop at the trash can didn't help at all, so he continued his odyssey to the bed before collapsing into it, shoes and all.

†††††††††††††††††††††††††

"CRIKEY, IT'S A GOOD thing Kent never sleeps," Chad mumbled, kicking a can as he turned the corner toward his new home. "I'd be a maggot if I woke him up at this hour, and anybody else would've been asleep ages ago."

He stopped short at the bottom of the stairs, sniffing the air. Smoke? That didn't seem right. Who in Florida had a fireplace? Sure, there might be a few weeks of freezing cold weather, but they were seldom consecutive and never enough to waste so much wall space. So why did the odor persist, and why was it getting stronger when he reached the door?

There was an overwhelming sense of doom flooding him as he touched the knob. It was hot to the touch, but thankfully, he had his gloves on. Smoke was curling through the edges of the window in dainty tendrils. Kent wasn't outside, but his truck was. All the lights were off inside. If Kent was home, he needed help.

"You in here, mate?" Chad choked as he spoke, the smoke burning his lungs and eyes. Yet despite the smokey haze, there was no flame visible anywhere. He turned his collar up and covered his mouth, then hurried inside.

Although he couldn't see anything, Chad had memorized the house—he had stubbed his toe on the end table in the hall once before committing the layout to memory. He could walk it blindfolded now; visibility wasn't the challenge. Breathing was. And if it was that bad for him after a few seconds, well, he didn't want to think about why Kent hadn't escaped.

"Kent?"

It wasn't just the smoke burning him now. The air hung hot and heavy; he knew he was nearing the source. It was getting harder to hold his breath with every passing second, to deny the most basic instinct, but breathing would be so much worse. If he could only hold on a few more seconds...Where was Kent? Why hadn't he made a sound? Hopefully, he had ridden with Jimmy, and they were out somewhere.

The hall seemed to be doubled in length, but he finally made it to Kent's door. The heat was so intense that he let out a pained squeak when he opened the door, even though he used his wool sleeve for added protection on the red-hot metal knob.

He had finally found the fire. After finding his way through the dim smoke, the flash of light was blinding, but his eyes quickly adjusted. The flames were licking the walls, and for a moment, he thought his friend had made it out safely.

It was only a moment. A low moan echoed through the room, barely audible over the crackling flames. At first, Chad thought it was the wood moaning, but instinct urged him on. He moved to check the bed—after all, why go to so much trouble and not go a few more steps? He could make it. Kent had done so much for him; the least he could do was walk to the bed.

And there he was. Kent was lying on the bed, his face contorted in pain, clutching his stomach and groaning pitifully.

"Come on, ya big yank!" Chad started trying to tug the detective to his feet. "We gotta go, mate!"

He had to support his friend almost entirely, but moved quickly, pausing to shut the door. Hopefully, that would hold the flames back a little longer. He kept trying to rouse Kent as they walked through the house, trying anything to snap his friend out of his trance.

Mere steps remained between him and the sweet air of freedom. It had been nearly impossible to navigate before, when he had a lungful of clean air and no dead weight. Could he make it? Or would they both die in a smoky stupor?

Chapter Three
The Escape

It felt like years, but Chad made it to the final obstacle: the front door. One more knob, and they'd be free. Once again he used his coat sleeve to protect himself from the glowing metal, and he turned it before half dragging Kent outside and down the stairs.

The crisp air flooded his lungs, almost making him giddy. Coughing as the smoke cleared his body, he glanced at Kent. His friend was doubled over, but seemed to be coming around. "Ya okay there, mate?"

Kent remained mute, wheezing and retching, but the house was in danger. There was no way the fire department would get there in time. Only one room was on fire now, but soon it would be the entire house. Chad knew where the extinguishers were, so he took a last gulp of fresh air before rushing back inside, the door again clicking closed behind him.

Although it took all four extinguishers, he soon put out the flames and began opening the back windows to let out the smoke. Many times he had laughed at his friend's paranoia. Four extinguishers for one house seemed excessive, and he really wasn't sure the new-fangled contraptions would be worth it. Now he understood, and his first purchase for the soon-to-be-renovated house would be four extinguishers for each room. After all, it had taken all four for Kent's bedroom, and he reasoned it was impossible to be too careful.

With the fire out, Chad stumbled to his room to open a window before practically falling down the trellis. If his head hurt after the brief trip to find Kent, it throbbed now. The fresh air soon worked its magic once again, and he made his way to the front of the house to check on the detective.

Kent hadn't moved since Chad had placed him safely out of harm's way; the detective was still rubbing his head and staring blankly at the house.

As soon as Chad finished clearing his lungs, he staggered to Kent. There was a small long-stemmed white rose that he hadn't noticed before, but that didn't keep his attention long. Kent was still watching the smoke oozing through the window frames.

Something wasn't right. Sure, Kent had been through a lot. Almost being burned alive would shock anybody into silence. But his eyes held no fear. They were dull and lifeless, staring stupidly at Chad's efforts to get a reaction.

Chad was getting worried. Kent kept mumbling and moaning, staring at something that wasn't there. Nothing seemed to help. The detective was so out of it that he didn't notice anything being said or done. Moments later, he clutched his stomach and collapsed to the ground.

That was enough. Although Chad knew Doris was a former nurse and often helped tend to their wounds, this seemed serious. This seemed like it warranted a hospital stay. Besides, would she even be available on such short notice, and so late at night? Could she handle whatever was ailing Kent? He wasn't sure, so he decided to call the O'Sullivans from the hospital. If that was the wrong choice, he knew she would tell him and have Kent discharged to her care.

His mind made up, he maneuvered the detective into the truck bed, then peeled off toward the hospital.

"Hey in there! Oi, we need some help out here."

Chad mashed the horn and shouted out the window. Kent had done nothing more than moan and mumble the entire trip, and he seemed to be getting worse. So, rather than waiting for help, Chad scrambled out of the truck's cab and half-carried the detective inside.

It only took one look before the admitting nurse had Kent wheeled away. Chad tried to relay what had happened, but how could he? He knew little more than the nurse. All he could say was that something must have incapacitated the detective before the fire had started, or he would have put it out himself.

Soon the police arrived, and Chad was left to answer questions with no answers. Unfortunately, the officer who came was a smug little man who despised Private Investigators and was thoroughly enjoying his perceived superiority. It was infuriating, and left Chad baffled. Kent did his job and did it well. Why was that being held against him?

Finally, Chad tired of the man's attitude and refused to talk anymore, instead hurrying to the phone. Within ten minutes, Jimmy and Doris had rushed inside, and another twenty minutes brought Lauren and her elderly roommate, Mrs. Williams.

The first thing Jimmy had done was call Kent's only friend on the force, Lieutenant Robert Sloane. Thanks to that phone call, Sloane arrived only minutes after Lauren, despite being confined to desk duty until he was completely recovered from his own brush with death. He quickly took control of the investigation, sending the other officer back to the station.

A short man came puffing past the officer, searching for Jimmy; a middle-aged blonde lady was running after him.

Jimmy started issuing orders when everyone arrived, beginning with the newest arrival. "Mac, ye best stand guard over Boss. We don't know who is responsible, so be vigilant. Mo ghrá, ye watch Boss and doctor on him; Miss Liza, ye can help me woman. Campbell, ye and Mrs. Williams start tidying the house back up. Lauren and I will look into Boss's new case; with any luck, we'll find out soon enough what he got himself into now. We'll start at the house while the cleaning crew goes to the hardware store. They'll not be open for hours, so best to look in me garage for starters. It might take some work to find, but there should be some putty and paint in there somewhere. I might even have some spare wood lying around from that shed Doris made me build last summer."

Lauren had an idea of her own. "If not, I have plenty of supplies at my home. William thought the entire house needed rebuilding rather than renovating, I suppose, and even with all of the work y'all have done, there is still plenty left over."

With that, the crew left, each to their own tasks.

The first thing Jimmy did was to study the ground. While Lauren was drawn to the rose that was so out of place, a metallic glint caught Jimmy's attention. Lying there on the ground was Kent's P38, bloodied and next to his dog tags. There were several broken bottles nearby, but besides the other signs of a struggle, there were no other clues.

Since there was nothing else to see outside, the pair moved indoors. The smoke still clung to the air, but the open windows had cleared it enough to be breathable. Unfortunately, that also meant the house was cold. Cold enough that neither even considered removing their gloves or coats.

They soon adjusted to the air; next, the condition of the house stole their attention. Although Kent always kept his house in a state of organized chaos, it was unrecognizable. The white panel walls were covered with soot, lending an eerie air to a normally welcoming house.

Still, there wasn't time to fret about what might have happened or cry about what did happen. And since she didn't want to worry about an ambush either, Lauren moved to lock the door.

Something made her pause when she touched it—a slight sticky feeling. Her glove had a strange, lotion-like residue on it, and she knew that could be a clue. Of course, it could also have meant that Kent had answered the door with aftershave on his hand, but she carefully turned her glove inside out, just in case.

With a sample safely stored, she got a rag and soap before cleansing the knob. If it had something to do with Kent's current condition, she wouldn't let anybody else get hurt by it. And if it wasn't, then that was one less thing her friends would have to clean.

Meanwhile, Jimmy had been searching the living room, the one room always clean in an otherwise messy house. Kent was always careful to keep it ready for company. He was also particular about which chair he used—he only had one tall enough to accommodate his height. So why was a comb in his chair?

Holding it up, Jimmy called Lauren over. "This is not me boyo's. And I cannot think of one person he would allow in his chair, unless this be yours. Yet 'twas wedged in the cushion there, so 'she', whoever 'she' be, left it there. Now to find out who 'she' is."

Lauren had said nothing, and Jimmy was studying her intently. "Cailín, ye be thinking of something that troubles ye. Oh, aye, I know ye be worried about Boss, as we all be, but ye were already upset when ye answered my call."

Lauren deflated. "It really is not important in the grand scheme of things."

"If it be bad enough to worry ye even with everything that has happened, it must be something important."

"Oh, fine. It isn't much, though."

"Cailín, enough. What is it?"

"Luke ended things. William saw this coming, but I truly did not. He was such a nice man, so God-fearing and thoughtful, but I suppose every man has his limits. He thought I spent too much time working, and that I was wrong for being so available to Kent.

"I tried explaining what a good friend William has been to me, even when he probably shouldn't have—when it could have killed him. William has always been there for me, ever since I first hired him. Luke said I was obsessed with him, and the relationship was inappropriate. He gave me a choice—can you believe it? Quit seeing him, or quit working with William. He said his wife would know her place, and not be working a man's job, especially one as vulgar as a detective's job. So I suppose you could say that I ended things. Nobody comes between me and my friends, and nobody gives me an ultimatum. And nobody, nobody, tells me what I can do. I enjoyed spending time with Luke, but not enough to end my life for him."

Jimmy's eyes, tired though they were, twinkled. "Sure and 'tis not me and mine ye would be missing, though."

"It most certainly would be!"

"Not like ye would miss him, though, and ye know it. He feels the same, ye know."

Lauren stared at him. "What do ye—I mean you—I mean, wait, what?"

"Ha! Ye sound like Mac. Ye know full well what I mean."

"He gave Luke his blessing—he practically introduced us."

"Lauren! He bought your da's bike, ignored his fear of crowds to go to church with ye, and 'tis ye alone can talk him back from the edge when no one else can. Ye even got him to promise to wait for backup."

"Which he obviously did not do."

"Which he does when possible. Ye be who he calls when the day is too much for him. He thinks he be too broken, and that he would only drag ye down with him."

"Nonsense!"

"Easy for ye to say. But is that how ye felt after being a prisoner in your home? After a few weeks? Imagine months of that. Besides, he has his own vanity, as do we all, and he fears letting ye see him. All he wants is whatever makes ye happy, and certain sure he sees only broken in the mirror. Now I have said my piece, and I'll say no more. To work ye'd best go, and we'll see if we cannot find what's happened to Boss."

A sudden noise interrupted their work. It was only four in the morning. There was no way Chad and Mrs. Williams had collected everything from the two homes already, even if they didn't wait for the hardware store to open. So who was at the front door?

Jimmy's hand immediately moved toward his pistol. Like Kent, he still carried his service weapon, although he had joined the Army before Pearl Harbor, so his weapon was older. Propped securely on his crutches, Jimmy discreetly readied himself to deal with the threat.

A loud knock echoed through the house, then two more. Without waiting for a response, the door swung open. "Detective-san, are you here? Is everything all right?"

Jimmy eased forward, but Lauren dodged him and placed herself between him and the intruder. "Who are you?"

Masao stopped and blinked. "I-I must be in the wrong place. My most humble apologies."

"You said detective. Is that who you were looking

for?"

"I apologize. This is the wrong house."

While Lauren was speaking, Jimmy had been thinking. He loathed everything the man standing in front of him represented, but Kent's behavior suddenly made sense. His mouth dropped. "Ye are Boss's new client."

Masao glanced between the two. "Hai."

His eyes narrowed as Jimmy spat, "Now it makes sense. Sure and he's been bothered for the last few days, but having ye as a client would have me as mad as a hatter. What I don't see is why he agreed to talk to ye in the first place."

Now Lauren's mouth dropped. Even when he was being tortured, she had never heard Jimmy speak with such hatred, and the anger of the two men charged the room with a palpable energy. She couldn't wait to get everything back to how it had been only moments before, when they didn't know the man existed. How had everything gone so wrong so quickly? Why was Jimmy so angry at someone he had never met? "Why wouldn't William just tell me—us—about you?"

"Bet I know."

"I am so sorry. He wanted only to spare you my troubles. This is most unfortunate, but I saw the rose outside—"

"Yeah, me too. And?"

"I come to him because of rose like that. Someone gave it to my daughter, and so he agreed to help me."

"That explains it. He said an innocent kid would get hurt if he stayed out of it. Sure and I knew he wouldn't say yes without cause."

Jimmy exhaled, trying to steady himself. Rage, pure rage, was fueling him as he tried to understand what had happened, what had brought this to his family. Well, there was no use dwelling on that now; he had inherited the case. For better or worse—much worse—he was going to have to take it, or whoever had tried to kill his friend and brother would be free to try again.

"Be there anything ye can think of that ye did not tell me boyo?"

Masao remained rigid, wincing as he inadvertently put pressure on his injured arm. "No, I regret to say there is no more."

Jimmy scowled. "Must be something, or ye wouldn't be here at this time o' day,"

Lauren laid her hand soothingly on his shoulder. "This was just an unexpected development, mister—?"

Masao attempted a bow, but stopped with a pained

grimace. "I am Masao Nagasaki. Your Detective-san was helping me."

"Well, Mr. Masao, what I don't understand is what you are doing here 'at this time of day.'"

"I received another rose an hour ago, with a note that if I stay any longer, I will end up like the Detective-san. I became worried and came to see if he was all right. Regretfully, it took time for me to find this place again. Where is he? Is he all right?"

"Yeah, no thanks to you."

"Hai, it is my fault. I apologize, and will trouble you no more."

Once again Lauren stepped up, but Jimmy motioned her away. "Boss took your case, and that be enough for me. And if it was your case that sent him to the hospital, sure and that be all the more reason for me to figure out who the sorry lot are. Nobody hurts my friend and bloody gets away with it. Did ye see who left the flower?"

Masao's eyes were too swollen to see Jimmy's doubtful expression, but he could hear the snicker in his voice when talking about the rose. Refusing to acknowledge the detective's mirth, he kept his voice even when replying. "I did not see who left it. I did not realize it until later, after I was awakened by a rock being thrown through my bedroom window."

He ruefully touched his temple, wincing and removing his hand as he revealed a fresh goose egg underneath his graying hair. "I know you believe me to be the enemy, and if I were completely honest, I would say the same of you. But for the sake of my family, I will work with anyone to keep them safe."

Jimmy relaxed slightly, shifting his weight from his aching legs to his muscular arms, relying more on his crutches. "All right, sure and I'd do the same for me own tykes. How old be the rugrats?"

Masao looked at him blankly, so Jimmy explained. "Kids, children. How old be your babes?"

"Hai, I understand now. My 'rugrats', as you call them, are ten, eight, and six."

"And from your tone, I'd guess daddy's little girl is six, hai?"

Masao nodded.

"Me little Rita is going on seven, so she be right between your two youngest. James Junior—we call him JJ—he be only five now, but 'tis sure a funny thing how they can turn your world upside down."

Again, Masao nodded.

"Look, Boss thought this was worth his time. 'Twas killing him, but he took it anyway. Where did they jump ye?"

"How did—why?"

"Not rocket science. Boss has been nursing some busted ribs, and ye look to have suffered similar injuries. Ye also seem as though ye could handle yourself, and I do not see me boyo jumping to your rescue unless the deck was stacked."

Lauren gasped, causing both men to turn toward her. "You were the cat!"

Seeing their confused expressions, she hurried to explain. "When I came to check on William a day ago, he began acting quite suspicious after there was a loud crash from the laundry room. He tried to explain it as the neighborhood cat, but he was so jumpy that I didn't fully believe him. You made the sound, didn't you?"

"Hai, I must have. I remember hearing him speaking with a woman, but when I tried to go investigate it, I misjudged the strength of the ironing board."

"Well, Mr. Masao Nagasaki, unless ye have anything else to say, ye best be off to rest in a hotel. It would not be a good idea to go to your home; if they are not finished with ye, they will know exactly where to find ye."

"I will not run. My neighbors hid, which has only made them more powerful. Someone must stop them, and I am no coward."

"What about your kids?"

"It is most important for them. They have been told by all they meet they are not worthy, and I refuse to have them grow up believing everyone is correct in that assumption. I will teach my children to stand their ground, and not to believe that just because someone who looks like you says they are worthless, it is true."

Jimmy chuckled. "Ye may not have noticed one little flaw in your rant. I may look like some folks around here, but nobody would hear me speak and think I am one. Me da survived the Black and Tans and Easter Rising, but decided Cork was no place to raise a family, since it did not seem like the Brits would be taking their boots off our necks. So da brought us here, but people never really trusted us, although the people here were much kinder than in other places. I never forgot where I came from, no matter how people laugh at me, or how many places say 'No Irish Need Apply, so ye can take your self-pity and shove it up your—"

Lauren laid her hand on his arm and shook her head; Jimmy took a deep breath, then kept talking. "Look, feel free to keep talking, since it only makes ye seem foolish. 'Tis a good look on ye."

"I apologize. But I must ask, would you teach your children to be cowards, or to stand up for themselves?"

"I would rather they learn from a safe distance and live to use what they learned. Have ye nowhere they could go?"

"My family stays together, and I am not..."

"A coward. Yeah, I got that part. If ye have naught else to say, I'd advise ye leave before somebody else finds ye here."

Jimmy couldn't wait for their uninvited guest to leave, and he turned to Lauren as soon as Masao was gone. "I understand why Boss took his case, and why it was eating at him so. Still, it be best to keep him as far away as possible from this."

Lauren sighed. "I understand this must be difficult for you, but—"

"'Tis not nearly so difficult for me as it be for Boss and Campbell. They spent months in a prison camp, and Campbell lost his brother to our rescue. Boss and I, when we first met, we fought Nazis. They caught me, and he only let them keep me for a few days before riding to me rescue. He did so good that they sent him off to fight a different war, and while we fought goose-steppers, he fought tunnels and kamikaze wackjobs. We cannot let Campbell find out about this and must keep Boss away from it, too. I cannot believe he would take this job—well, I do, but I don't. But Boss is going to need ye there when he wakes up."

"But-but I'm working with you!" Lauren sputtered, unable to believe that Jimmy was brushing her off too. She expected that from Kent, but Jimmy? This was too much. "Mac, Mrs. O'Sullivan, and Liza Jane are all there to tend to him. I can help, even if your overprotective mother hen of a friend thinks I should stay home and knit."

"Look, cailín, Boss is trying to keep ye safe. I know 'tis frustrating, to be sure, for sure and he does the same thing to me, but his heart be in the right place. And now he be needing ye, not me, not Mac, no, nor even me spitfire of a wife. He needs someone from his present to pull him out of his hole, not his past. We would only remind him more of where he's been. Ye can help him like none of us can."

Lauren wasn't convinced and still thought Jimmy was giving her the runaround, but she grudgingly obliged. Honestly, it stung that Jimmy didn't trust her enough to let her work with him once it started to look tough. After all the time and effort he'd spent training her, now he was just going to bench her? They were a protective bunch—she'd known that from the start—but she had hoped that she could prove to them she was just as capable as they were. Now, she finally had her chance, and she was getting sent to safety! And Jimmy, of all people, should know better. He said that she was the best pupil he'd ever had—and although she doubted he'd trained many people, that still felt like a compliment. Was he just patronizing her? Why else would he be so eager to get rid of her?

She was still muttering angrily when she skulked into the hospital, but came to a screeching stop when she saw Mac. Something didn't seem quite right. Samuel McDonald was loyal and loveable, but not athletic. If there was a chair within a hundred miles, you would find Mac sitting in it. And although he meant well, if he was sitting down, even if he was on guard, he was going to fall asleep. So why was he pacing, completely oblivious to the chair positioned neatly by Kent's door?

Lauren wasn't trying to sneak up on him, but Mac jumped when she spoke to him, then silently motioned to Kent's room before beginning to pace again. His normally jovial face was lined with worry, and no matter how hard she tried, he remained mute. Since he was never silent, the encounter only made her more nervous about what she was about to find.

Still, Mac got worked up easily. Although she was shaken, Lauren opened the door confident that Kent would laugh at her for being such a worrywart.

What she saw was as far from reassuring as possible. Doris was rocking anxiously in a chair next to his bed, despite the chair having legs and not rockers. The result was that each tilt of the chair left her perilously close to tipping over, yet she was so engrossed in studying the detective that she remained oblivious.

That led Lauren's gaze to the bed. Any thoughts of this being a wasted trip instantly vanished, and she felt a twinge of guilt that she had been forced to come. Her robust friend, whose skin was so well tanned it bordered on being leathery, had yellow flesh so thin it resembled onion peeling. A strange garlic odor hung heavily in the room, and his jagged, shallow breaths did little to convince anyone that he was still alive.

Lauren stood there, transfixed, for several moments. An especially labored breath startled her out of her reverie, and she moved silently to Doris, laying her hand on the older woman's shoulder.

As jumpy as Mac was, Doris was even worse. She almost flipped her chair over in fright as she hurried to see who the intruder was, clutching her throat. "You gave me such a fright! I was nae expecting anyone. Were ye nae to be helping my husband suss out what happened at Billy's?"

Lauren wilted under the scrutinizing stare, but

remembered Jimmy's instructions. Nobody, not even Doris, was to find out about Kent's newest client. Sounded simple enough.

<u>Sounded</u> simple. Doris O'Sullivan was one of the most perceptive people that Lauren had ever met. To survive a secretive, trouble-prone group like Jimmy, Mac, and Kent, she had to be. It worked great for Doris, but not so much for anybody trying to hide something from her. Yet although her task was easier said than done, Jimmy said it was the right thing to do, and Lauren trusted him implicitly. So, no matter how hard it would be, she would just have to figure out a way to convince Doris that she was being truthful.

The best way to do that was to stay as close to the truth as possible. "Jimmy sent me to check on William. Nobody had called us with an update yet, and he didn't want to risk waking him up if he was sleeping. Since he was doing paperwork, there was nothing more pressing for me to do, so I came to see him in person. Now I want to know what is happening. From what Chad said, I expected he would be nearly recovered by now. I thought he had suffered a beating and smoke inhalation. None of that explains why he, well, what, I mean, he should not be..."

"Oh, aye, that's true. He did get beaten and nearly

turned into a Billy pancake, but Billy boy, he does nothing halfway. Nae him! They say that from the look of him, he has been beat nae once, but twice! And as if that wasn't enough, he got himself trapped in a fire. But although that would be enough for any sane person to give up and lick their wounds, do you think Billy would be happy with such trivial inconveniences?"

She paused for a moment, but continued without letting Lauren speak. "All the ways he has nearly kicked it over the years, and he still managed to find a new way to die. He just had to one-up himself."

Lauren huffed. She expected this rambling from Mac, but Doris should have explained herself by now. "Mrs. O'Sullivan, please."

"Oh, be patient, lass. I'm getting there. 'Tis another first he's gone and done and 'tis that reason that he's in such bad shape. This time, he's been poisoned. T'was the smell that tipped them off—he came in smelling like he had been fighting off vampires. Did you know that's a sign of arsenic? I did nae. But if he ever turns up smelling like he's been hiding in an Italian's spice rack again, you can believe that I'll be prepared. If the sod hadn't remembered they were dealing with a giant, or had they planted the trap for Jimmy, I would be planning a funeral now. Luckily, they did nae factor that into their scheme, and they did nae know he is too stubborn to go toes up, aren't you, Billy boy?"

Doris lovingly squeezed his hand, shuddering at the raspy breath that answered her. She furiously swiped away a tear that dared to race down her cheek, then charged out of the room.

Alone with her friend for the first time, Lauren was in shock. What should she say? He didn't seem to have heard anything that had been said before. Doris was right; he had come too close to death too many times for this to be any different. He was the closest thing to Superman she had ever seen, surviving bullets and knives with only a scar to remember them by. Surely he'd walk away from this. He had to.

Lauren leaned over and clasped Kent's hand to her cheek before whispering to him. "William, you cannot do this to me. You never quit, so don't you dare start now! I chose you, William. Do you hear me? Luke made me choose, and I chose you. I hope you listen to me, William. Now, you have a choice, and you better choose right. If you have one single decent bone in your body, you'll choose to come back. Just come back, William. So help me, if you don't, if you die on me—well, I'll never forgive you. Do you understand me? You better come back. I plan to spend my New Year's with you, and you better be here to see it."

Was she imagining things? He was still so fragile, so motionless, but she could swear that she heard, "I will."

Chapter Four
The Undesirables

Jimmy had studied the battle scars left in the sand so many times he still saw it when he closed his eyes. He had taken pictures of everything with the pocket camera Kent had gotten him for Christmas—even Kent's blood-stained P38, lying partially buried under the sand.

With that done, he collected the bottles—with the fingerprints they held—and moved back inside. "Aye, that'll even things up. Sure and I'll get some answers out of Boss yet, even if he won't tell me anything. Closed-mouthed as he is, I might even get better answers without him."

Being alone never stopped Jimmy from having a conversation. He was a sociable person. Besides, as he often told Doris, 'Sometimes, it be nice to talk to someone with good sense'. It was something familiar, and he yearned for the comfort of familiarity. This case was bringing him into unfamiliar territory; for once, he was taking a case personally. That never happened to him. Sure, he might get insulted sometimes and react, but to let a case get so far under his skin? That was Kent's specialty. Jimmy was the one people underestimated, the jolly jokester they didn't see coming. But he was also methodical and used whatever he had as a weapon, including his laughing nature. Right now, he needed to talk through his ideas. So, alone or not, he was going to talk.

"Boss, why do ye keep doing this to me? Make me keep searching for answers to questions I do not know—it be most unfair of ye to keep putting me in this spot. And leaving me with this case was downright rotten of ye, and sure and I'll make ye pay for this one, me boyo. Now, where to look..."

Jimmy thought he knew all of Kent's hiding places. They were for security from outsiders, not him. He had his own hiding spots, and the two would use them for communications. Yet even after searching each of them, he hadn't found anything helpful. He found nothing, even when he thumbed through the Irish book of poems where they hid notes.

With every spot searched, he began looking for new

compartments. Kent had become fascinated with them while working for Lauren almost two years before. That was when he had realized he needed better security. Thanks to Lauren's house, he had ample opportunities to study hidden cubbyholes. Unfortunately for him, Jimmy had seen those same hidden doors, also knew how his friend thought. It didn't take long for him to find a hidden compartment in the bottom of the coffee table drawer, and it took even less time to translate Kent's shorthand. After all, they both learned it from Doris.

A quick glance at the notes proved Masao had told the truth, but there wasn't much more written on the pages. From what Jimmy read, Kent hadn't gotten much farther than he himself had, and he had only been on the job for a few hours. In fact, in an ironic twist of fate, the attack on Kent had moved the case farther than anything else, providing the fingerprints to identify everybody involved. But knowing that, it made no sense that his friend had been targeted.

"Well, sure and that copper should be back to his work by now. Maybe he can help."

Jimmy drove to the station in an extremely uncharitable mood. He knew that, as soon as he walked inside, he'd be a double target—one for who he was, and one for what he did. He didn't have the time or patience to put up with that. So he stopped at a phone booth and called Sloane, just to make sure he wasn't about to go behind enemy lines alone.

The dial tone droned as he entered his change and waited to be connected with the police detective. "Do ye recognize who this be, Lieutenant?"

Sloane answered slowly, thinking hard as he formed his answer. "Yeah, the Irishman...O'Sullivan, right?"

Although Jimmy would've bristled at the condescending tone that usually accompanied that statement, he knew the man was still recovering, and had difficulty with names. Since Jimmy had lost ten years to his own memory problems, he was very sympathetic to anyone in a similar situation. "Ay, that be me. I spoke to ye a few hours ago, and I've got meself a lead I need help with. Seems like the last time they beat Boss was right in front of his own front door, and they were glaikit—foolish—enough to leave behind incriminating evidence. Sure and I'd be appreciating it if ye would run their prints for me, so I can know whose—ahem, rear—to kick for hurting me brother."

"I oughta report that as a credible threat," Sloane chuckled, knowing firsthand the damage Jimmy could do. "'Course, I'm not usually considered reliable around here anymore. Maybe they're right—I might not've even heard what you said exactly right. Get me your prints and I'll run 'em. How is, um..."

Hearing Sloane rummaging through his notes again, Jimmy interrupted to answer. "Me boyo, Kent? I'm sure he will be right as rain in two shakes of a lamb's tail. I can do no more for him than mo ghrá, but I can figure out who did this to him and keep them from finishing the job."

"Right—Kent. I'll help any way that I can."

"The fingerprints should be more than enough for now, and I do thank ye."

With that, Jimmy hung up and began working again. It didn't take long to leave the prints with Sloane and return to Kent's, but he had learned all the house had to tell. Now it was time for his least favorite task: knocking on doors.

It went as slowly as he expected. This neighbor was at work, this one was a mother with twins who only wanted her babies to finish their naps. Yes, she had heard a commotion around eleven. It had woken her children up and she looked forward to eventually telling off everyone involved, but at the moment, she had better things to do than get involved in somebody else's problems.

Having vented, she quickly slammed the door in Jimmy's face, making it time to visit the next home—another failure. After that came another empty home, this one with a stuffed mailbox. If the dates were to be believed, nobody had been there for at least two weeks, so after making sure there were no squatters inside, Jimmy moved on to the next house. And so on, so on, and so on. The houses weren't close to each other but were all within sight of Kent's house, and the night had been a quiet one. The irate mother had heard the argument, but somehow, nobody else had. That was annoying enough, but the looks he got were infuriating. Everything in him screamed to wipe the pitying, self-satisfied smirks off their faces. Instead, he bit down on his tongue, filling his mouth with the familiar metallic taste of blood, but doing little to calm him.

As he walked back to Kent's, he knocked on the doors that had been closed to him before. Most stayed silent, hoping he would leave, but a few more were opened to him.

One such door opened to reveal a bony old woman, her spectacles at the end of her hawkish nose. As she looked over the black-rimmed glasses, she sniffed contemptuously. "Well?"

Although taken aback by the woman's abrupt manner, Jimmy flashed a dazzling smile. "Well, ye see, ma'am, I was wanting to know—"

"What happened at that hooligan's house? I don't know why you don't just ask your friend."

"How did ye...?"

She snorted as she looked down at him. "I live here alone, so I make it my business to keep myself safe. With neighbors like your friend, it pays to watch carefully. I see you and your family visit there, and may I just say that you seem like too nice a bunch to associate with such trash, but I suppose that is your business. Still, bringing children to a house with such filth. You should be ashamed! And that beating was no more than he deserved, interrupting the peace of my night by bringing a trollop to his house! So indecent. If I had my say, he'd be tarred and feathered, then run out of town on a rail. That's just my opinion, but children really have no business being in a place where such riffraff congregates."

Two different emotions were fighting inside Jimmy. The nosy neighbor was so self-righteous and full of condemnation that his supreme desire was to make her choke on her words. Yet hidden away inside the bile was a clue, and an important one at that. For the first time,

Jimmy had a rough timeline of what had happened. The mystery woman who left the comb in Kent's chair had come hours before the thugs attacked him at eleven, and Campbell had come back to the smoking room at midnight.

Who had set the fire? It couldn't have been long before the Aussie returned, or Kent would have been dead and the house burned to the ground. The remnants of a Molotov cocktail had been in the bedroom, and even this nosy busybody couldn't have seen the arsonist from her post.

Still, the nosy shrew could probably tell him everything else that had happened that night. Even better, she wanted to talk! His only problem was to keep silent long enough to hear everything she had to say. As angry as he was, that would not be easy. He hoped reminding himself not to hit a woman would be enough to keep calm.

"There be some shady folks who visit and 'tis no more than the truth you've said there. I was wondering, though, if ye happened to get a good look at the floozy? Sure and she may be up to no good, trying to sweet talk her way in before setting up house, and neither ye nor I want that. If ye help me find her, certain sure and I'll see to it she never comes back again."

The old woman cackled gleefully. Finally, someone was taking her seriously. "Well, young man, I knew I liked you for a reason. Even if you come from questionable heritage, you seem to have your head on straight. I wish I could help more, but I didn't get a good look at her. She had a silk scarf covering her hair, a cashmere coat, leather driving gloves, and those cat-eye sunglasses that are so popular now. Late as it was, being after dark and all, she used them to hide who she was. Probably some married woman slipping around on her husband, and him probably off fighting, thinking she's a good girl."

She snorted, and her nose wrinkled like she smelled something bad. "He looked surprised to see her, but your friend sure let her inside in a hurry. Must've been his conscience bothering him. They didn't waste any time, either; I bet it wasn't six minutes later that she was coming out, trying to put her gloves back on. Your friend must've gotten her quite worked up, because she ended up putting them in her purse instead of bothering with them. The indecency of your friend is appalling, and I hope you see that now, and don't bring those innocent children to him for further corruption."

Jimmy once again tasted blood, but clenched his fists to keep from lashing out at her. "I'm sorry ye did not see her better. Did ye see her car, perchance?"

The busybody chuckled. "She didn't want to be recognized, that's for sure. Startled me when she popped up on his doorstep, like she appeared out of nowhere. But you can bet your bottom dollar I watched her until she was out of sight. Yes, sir! She parked way up the street, three houses down at least, and drove for a block before she turned on her lights."

Jimmy couldn't hide the disappointment in his voice. "So ye did not get a good look at her car, either?"

The old woman clicked her tongue, her jutted jaw making a bony click with each move. "Did I say that? You don't have much patience, do you? Just like everybody else, in a rush. That's the problem with you young folks these days. In such a hurry to find out you don't take the time to listen to what's right in front of you. In my day, we respected our elders. Why, I would never have been so rude as to presume to interrupt somebody with so much more experience in life!

"Of course I saw her car. I'm not blind! It was one of those station wagons that was popular a few years back—the ones with all the wood on them. Hah! Always thought anybody who used 'em was nuts. All that work to get away from buggies, and some idiot turns a buggy into a car. Guess that's part of what made them so cheap; there wasn't enough metal on 'em to make 'em cost much.

"How somebody could afford a coat like she had on but drive such a plain car I'll never understand. I suppose her sap of a husband is too busy paying for her wardrobe to afford the simple luxuries of life.

"I thought that was the end of it until I heard a crash a few hours later. Woke me up and nearly scared me to death! I thought somebody was breaking down my front door, but I'm so glad I got to see it! His indiscretion came back to bite him, and I will go to my grave thanking the good Lord for letting me see it!

"After the crash, your friend _finally_ came out to see what happened. One of 'em was waiting on the porch for him and shoved him down the stairs. Honestly, it surprised me it took him so long to investigate! Usually, he's outside before the sound from the crash even has time to reach my ears, and don't get me started on the fourth of July. And the way he stumbled out the door told me exactly why he took so long. Wouldn't you know he was drunk? And he never even saw it coming."

She waggled a skeletal finger knowingly. "I couldn't have dreamed a more fitting comeuppance. After all the things he's gotten away with, the Klan finally came to visit as a reward for his ill-chosen company. Maybe he'll take the hint and keep the undesirables away from his house now."

Jimmy's jaw dropped. "Klan with a K?"

"Yes, sir! They started setting the cross up, but he interrupted them. Or maybe they wanted him to watch, since there was one on the porch waiting for him. They didn't have a chance to finish before they left, though. It's a pity—if they could only have finished the cross, everybody would finally see that I'm right. We might even have gotten rid of him."

"How many men was it, then?" His voice was harsh, but Jimmy couldn't help it. The bigoted woman was well past his tolerance level for stupidity; there was only one reason she didn't have a broken jaw, and that was her gender; even her age wouldn't have been able to save him from his wrath at this point. He could only hope she was so self-absorbed that she wouldn't hear his jaw grinding.

Luck was on his side, and she prattled merrily on. "Oh, it must've been about eight of 'em."

"Why did they have to leave?"

"Well, and mind you, I couldn't see very well from inside my house, but it looked to me like he fought them off. I don't know how—he never got up from his trip down the stairs, but they started screaming and limping away with slashed robes, so I can only assume he fights dirty. In my day, men fought by the rules and didn't bring a knife to a fistfight."

"And in me day, people be smart enough to realize there be innocent brawls where ye use fisticuffs and then there be fighting for the very air ye breathe. And when ye be fighting for your life, ye do not just lay there and hope that somebody has mercy on ye and stops trying to kill ye. What's more, even busybodies know there be a difference between fighting to the death and a fistfight. If it be the former, decent folk stay to help, or at least call for help. And decent folk keep an eye out for their neighbors not to judge them and gossip, but to help them when they need it. In me day, people don't kick somebody for helping someone in need, they don't crow when a genuine hero gets ambushed and nearly killed just for helping people nobody else cares about, and their minds be not so far in the gutter that they assume something foul from a six-minute visit. And finally, in me day, people would not be associating with nosy old hags with no better way to spend their time than to invent malicious lies and hope they take root. Ye have a good day, ma'am."

Jimmy tipped his hat before limping away as defiantly as his weary legs could manage, leaving the old woman shaking with anger. Despite feeling somewhat relieved that he had spoken up for his friend, Jimmy's wrath was blazing hot, and he had no one to unleash it on.

His arms were sore from the extra walking and his back ached, but he was too angry to notice. He soon made it across the sandy road and limped stiffly up the stairs before moving to Kent's bedroom, too infuriated to notice that someone was calling him.

As he closed the door, the car pulled into Kent's garage. Chad climbed out and began unloading the materials he had gathered over the day. He debated going after Jimmy, but decided to wait until his friend had calmed down. There was enough work to keep him busy for several minutes, and he hoped that would be long enough.

Even though he was frustrated that it had taken him so long to get started, Chad was grateful for the nap Mrs. Williams had forced on him. He had been tired when he arrived home from his walkabout, and she had seen that. The result was a four-a.m. shower and a meal followed by a three-hour nap, which was refreshing but had cost precious time. He wanted to get the house ready for Kent's return, and the cleanup hadn't started yet.

Mrs. Williams began stacking buckets of paint to carry upstairs, and he begrudgingly resigned himself to the fact that he was about to become a carpenter and a painter. As much fun as watching paint dry sounded, he was thankful that he still had two days off. Maybe he wouldn't have that much to do. If he was really lucky, it would only take a day to get everything fixed up. After all, it was only smoke damage and one broken window.

A dull splintering sound forced its way through the door, and both dropped their supplies and hurried inside. It took Chad only moments to sprint up the stairs and kick open the wooden door, and even less time to track the sound. His heart pounded in his ears as he opened the bedroom door, half-expecting a repeat of the previous night. What if it was? Should he have helped Jimmy clear the house instead of giving him time? Surely that had already been done. And where was Lauren? Had she been taken?

When the door swung open, Chad's pistol was drawn, but he wasn't ready for what awaited him. Jimmy was shaking his hand, but there was nobody there.

There was the answer. It wasn't a person who had fallen victim to Jimmy's right hook, but the wall. This job was definitely going to take longer than a day now.

The fist-sized hole in the wall explained the hand and the sound, but not Jimmy's mood.

"Jimmy?"

Jimmy looked at him, his eyes still black with rage, an expression Chad easily recognized. The question was, what had made him so angry?

Suddenly, the answer hit him. Jimmy's assignment was finding answers, and interviewing neighbors would have been part of that. "Ya talked to that old stickybeak across the way, didn't ya?"

No answer, but Jimmy blinked slowly, his pupils returning to normal as he pondered the question.

"Ya did, didn't ya? Is she still breathing?"

When Jimmy nodded slowly, Chad chuckled. "Yeah, she makes me feel that way, too. Good on ya for not putting her down, mate. I've had that urge meself. Keeps peeking out her window, waiting for something to happen, and comes over at all hours to complain about one thing or another. Once her cat went missin', and she came over, blamin' Kent for it. Another time, the wind got up and blew over a bunch of stuff. She stormed over to accuse him of that, too. He tried pointing out all the damage and reminded her it was a regular gale, but she wouldn't hear of it. She stacked her stuff right. No way it was subject to the same laws of physics everybody else lives by. She lives to spread misery, mate. Don't let her eat at ya so."

Jimmy nodded slightly, still rigid, but his breathing was slowly returning to normal. "It is not right, what she said about Boss, but ye be right. Have ye heard anything about how Boss be?"

"No, have you?"

"'Tis not like mo ghrá; maybe she called while I was out."

Thankful for the distraction, Jimmy nodded at Mrs. Williams, standing silently in the doorframe, before hobbling to the phone.

To his surprise, there was no sound. He clicked the receiver a few times, but still nothing. Nobody else was using the line, but there was no dial tone.

Mumbling an apology to his confused friends, Jimmy limped out the back door to the box outside. Picking up the wire dangling loosely from its perch, he tapped the wall thoughtfully. "Now who would go and cut his phone line?"

He soon had spliced the wires well enough for the phone to work again and finished placing his call.

Noticing the worried expression on Chad's face, he offered a halfhearted explanation. "She probably called several times by now, to say Boss be all right. Sure and she's probably worked herself into a tizzy, not being able to get hold of me.

"Hiya, mo ghrá, how be ya?"

His forced cheerfulness evaporated as Doris unleashed her anger on him. She was tired and worried, and her husband's chipper voice was all it took to give her a reason to unleash her fury. "Oh, 'how be ye?', Because I have nae been worrying about you for the last five hours. Where have you been? You sent Lauren back, but I have nae been able to reach you. Do you not think that I have enough to be worried about? Because you are nae here, it does nae matter. I 'be' at the hospital holding vigil for poor Billy, but it sounds like you are having a grand old time. Is that why I have nae heard from you? I supposed as much. Trust you lot to get sucked into a fool's errand. 'Tis not enough that Billy is lying here fighting for his life, but you are dead set on joining him! Can you nae take the hint? Whatever he is doing should be left alone. I will nae let this happen to you, too. You have children and a wife, but do nae let that stop you. You have a mystery to solve."

A dial tone followed the loud thud from the other end. Now Jimmy was more worried than ever. How had he upset her so quickly? He assumed she had used him as a whipping boy for the same reason he had used

Kent's wall as a punching bag. He had a good reason for knocking a hole in it. What was her reason for lashing out at him?

He was smart enough to give her a few minutes before calling back. "Now, mo ghrá, me heart, me love, me woman, what be wrong? I be fit as a fiddle, and Boss is always okay in the end. Sure and ye will see. Everything will be fine, just as always."

"Maybe..." Doris stopped herself. Telling Jimmy that his friend had been poisoned would only make him work harder to solve the case, and that was the last thing she wanted.

"Doris, what be it? What be troubling ye?" Jimmy asked gently.

Silence.

"Leannán?"

"I'm here." Doris sighed. "I'm just so very, very tired."

He heard the tremble in her voice and knew there was more she wasn't telling him. Tenderly, he kept pushing. "What be wrong?"

She stayed silent.

"Mo chroí! Ye are hiding something. What?"

"Billy is—it's not good, James."

Fear gnawed at his gut, but he refused to let it take over. "Boss is fine. He will be fine—always is."

"Well, this is different. This time he went and got himself poisoned."

The stunned detective fell back into empty air, completely missing the chair. Chad panicked as he slid a seat underneath Jimmy before he could hit the floor, but even after his leg connected with the wooden bottom of the seat, Jimmy remained oblivious.

Chad waited for an explanation, but received none. He had only heard half of the conversation, and the phone was still dangling uselessly from Jimmy's hand. Even if Jimmy wouldn't give him an answer, he could still get one from Doris. "Doris! What did ya say to get Jimmy so worked up?"

"Is he all right?"

"Yeah, just got the wind knocked out of him is all. What's the matter with Kent?"

"Somebody slipped him some arsenic. They aren't sure exactly when, other than it happened sometime yesterday afternoon or evening. It would nae have killed him otherwise, since the auld mahoun only used enough to kill me, nae him. But add in the beatings and smoke inhalation, plus the poison had time to work—well, it just doesn't look good."

"He's a tough bloke."

"Aye, but is he tough enough?"

Chad had no answer for that and hung up.

Only the sound of the receiver clicking roused Jimmy, who glanced up with an embarrassed smile. "Reckon I swooned like a schoolgirl. Did she tell ye more than I let her tell me?"

"Aw, mate, she's worried. 'Bout you and Kent. Sound of it, don't think she holds much hope for him."

"She still thinks like a civilian. All these years, she hasn't gotten rid of that habit. It isn't the same with him, and ye know it as well as I do. If that camp could not break him, sure and there be no way this can. I doubt anything short of the angel Azrael himself could claim Boss."

"Well, one of ya is right, but I ain't gettin' in the middle of that. Just a good thing I came back when I did."

"Yeah, about that. I thought ye were going to stay gone another two days. What brought ye back?"

"Dunno. It was just a feelin' I had that somethin' wasn't right. Got here and smelled smoke, then seen it comin' out the windows. The fire hadn't spread through the house yet; it was still just in his room, but Kent was just lyin' in his bed, starin' at the ceilin' and moanin'. I didn't see anythin' else outta the ordinary, but after I finished inside and came back out, I found him starin' at the house. It was weird, like he was somewhere else. For just a second he came back, but then he was gone again."

Jimmy had learned everything the house had to offer except the intruders' identities. The arsonist had left behind a trail of sand but no footprints, and he had finished reading the case notes. Now that he had Chad's statement, there was nothing left for him to do. He left Chad and Mrs. Williams to their work and returned to the station, hoping it had been long enough for Sloane to find something.

Once again Jimmy phoned before going inside. He was ready, willing, and able to take his frustrations out on anybody in his path; facing a lot of unfriendly cops seemed like a bad idea. One would mouth off, and with the mood he was in, the unfortunate man would end up being a punching bag. That would definitely end badly, so it was best he be careful.

Thankfully, Lieutenant Sloane was in. By the time Jimmy walked through his door, the stack of files was waiting on his desk. "Irish..."

"Me name is Jimmy." He felt bad for making Sloane his target; as angry as he was, he still remembered that the policeman meant nothing by it. But he was out for blood, and since he had been so careful to avoid everybody else, he was stuck.

"Right. Jimmy. I've got your—these things that you asked for. How is, um, you know, he?"

"Boss'll be fine. Takes more than that to put down William Kent. Thanks."

Jimmy limped out to his car, which he promptly swapped for Kent's truck. If somebody was watching, he wanted them to think Kent was still on the job. He also didn't want them to trace his home through his car.

It had been too long since he had slept, and the adrenaline was wearing off. He wasn't any good to anybody right now, and he wanted to be at his best. That meant it was time to find somewhere secluded and take a nap.

An hour later, Jimmy was wiping the drool from the corner of his mouth and trying to stretch. The short siesta had helped; now he was eager to see what Sloane had found.

The files were thorough, giving faces to each fingerprint that Jimmy had found. None of the goons were over twenty, but each already had the makings of a hardened criminal. A few were even suspected of murder, but somehow evaded the chair no matter how strong the charges against them were.

This didn't make sense. None of them seemed smart

enough to get away with shoplifting a pair of socks, so how were they getting away with murder? All the file told him was that they knew each other, and not a criminal mastermind who could keep them out of trouble. And they didn't have any association with the Klan, so why had they shown up in white robes? They seemed to hate everybody equally, which killed the supposed motive of racism.

He found one useful thing in the files. Tucked neatly in all the paperwork was their favorite hangout, and the abandoned pool hall they called home wasn't far away.

The first time, he drove past the building, looking for any sign of an ambush and a good place to hide Kent's '56 Chevy that wasn't too far away. Only three cars in the driveway; that looked promising. And only a quarter mile away was a dilapidated shed with plenty of room to camouflage the truck. It was farther than he wanted to walk, but he could handle the sand that far. He had a lifetime of being kicked around to fuel him on; every slur that had ever been thrown at him was harnessed into justice for his friend. If that meant he had to maneuver his crutches through the sand for a few minutes, he would.

Finally, he made it to the door. Even in the forty-degree weather, Jimmy's jacket was wet with sweat, but at least now his crutches were on even ground.

One breath, two. His pistol was drawn and ready. He had the element of surprise and was counting on that edge to level things if all eight were inside.

There was something wrong. Despite the cars outside, everything inside was as silent as a graveyard at midnight. Were they expecting him? Had the fingerprints been a plant so they could lure Kent, or his replacement, there? That would certainly change the fight dynamics.

Well, it didn't matter. Honestly, it might make it a fair fight. He was a boxer. The crutches slowed him down in some ways, but he had designed them himself to help with his fights. They were heavier than most, and designed to break in half at the push of a button. The left crutch revealed a gun, and the right a knife, while the shoulder rests on both had curved steel underneath the pads. If it came to it, they would serve as an excellent blunt force object.

Not that it had ever gotten that far. Since he had started working as a detective, he had been ambushed exactly twice, and the crutches couldn't help either time. He had used the experiences to tweak them, and this was his chance to test his invention and vent his anger all at once.

He listened carefully. Another quiet breath, but still not a sound in the house. No squeaking floorboards, no whispers, nothing. Seven breaths, then eight. *Well, might as well get it over with.*

Bracing, Jimmy got ready to break open the door, but tested the knob first. Surprise—it turned. No time for second-guessing, to think about Doris, to turn around and wait for backup. Now was the time for action.

Jimmy studied the floor for any signs of weakness. None were visible. A quick glance in the hall mirror didn't show anyone hiding, but that wasn't a guarantee.

His first step in was silent. So were the next six. And despite having almost made it to the backroom, there was still no sign of an ambush. There was a table with an ashtray on it, the remains of something that had been burned beyond recognition, but there were still no other signs of life.

Opening the last door, he finally discovered why. Seven bodies would turn the nicest resort into a morgue, but in this place, it was downright eerie. Bloody rags littered the floor, telling a story he couldn't believe. The thugs were just kids—in person, there was no denying their youthfulness; a few of them didn't even look old enough to shave.

Jimmy blinked. It had been a long time since he saw this many bodies. Twelve years, eight months, and three days, to be exact. That didn't matter. The smell of death brought it all flooding back like it was only yesterday.

A sweeping glance was enough to confirm that the boys were dead, but Jimmy methodically moved by each and felt for a pulse. They couldn't have been dead long; despite the chill in the air, the bodies were still warm to the touch.

Before he had finished checking the young men, he heard something from behind another door.

He crept toward the sound. His pulse was racing so fast that his head was throbbing, and he was having trouble seeing clearly. He needed to punch something to let off steam soon. All the friends that he couldn't save who were now lying in the ground, all the men he had put there himself; they all flashed in front of him. *Not now, I do not have time for ye. Go torment someone else and let me do me job.*

One last steadying breath to chase off the ghosts and he flung open the door, pistol ready.

Lying on the ground was the eighth attacker. His breaths were shallow, and there was no mistaking the rattle coming from his body.

Jimmy awkwardly kneeled next to the dying teen and put a hand on his shoulder.

"I-I'm so col-cold. Wh-why?"

"Well, garsún, you're dying," Jimmy said gently.

"N-no, wh-why, I wasn-wasn't going to-to talk. Why?"

Another breath, jagged and long, then silence.

Out of habit, Jimmy checked the teenager's pulse, even though he knew what he'd find. He quietly closed the youth's eyes and did the sign of the cross over him, then began searching for clues and photographing everything.

His first clue was from the dead kid. 'I wasn't gonna talk.' Somebody had killed him to shut him up; somebody had been there to tie up loose ends. Was that why the other room felt so staged?

That's what was bothering him. Seven kids got their arteries slashed by one barely conscious detective, drove fourteen miles, bandaged themselves, removed the bandages, then just sat down and waited to bleed out. But how could somebody have forced seven people to sit around and wait for death? And why beat the last one to death? Finally, how many men did it take to kill eight people, even if only one had been uninjured?

Jimmy smiled as he kept using his pocket camera. He had laughed at Kent for getting it, then laughed harder when he found another under the tree with the name tag 'Jimmy' on it. Until mere hours before, he only appreciated it as a gadget to tinker with and study. He had never dreamed it would come in handy.

He would have to remember to thank his friend for it later, but right now, he needed to document everything. No matter how badly wounded Kent was, Jimmy knew the cops would find out who caused the initial wound—i.e. William Kent—and decide that the case was closed. Sure, Sloane would probably try to help him, to convince everyone else to find the truth, but things were how they were. Hardly anybody at the station took the policeman seriously right now. They thought that his occasional struggle with words and constant forgotten names made him damaged goods. Johnstone might step in, but his promotion was recent enough that he was worried about jeopardizing his job.

If anyone was going to solve this case, it would have to be done before the police got involved, or at least before they pinned it on Kent. And the way things were looking, that somebody would have to be him.

Jimmy photographed every inch of both rooms before touching anything, then carefully looked for anything that might be a clue. Nearly everything was gone; only the paper in the ashtray had been left. It was destroyed, so it must've been important, but why burn it? Why not take it with them? Surely the teenagers hadn't stopped dying long enough to destroy evidence, but why hadn't their killers done a better job getting rid of it? Just leaving the remnants was a mistake, and if they had made one, they had made another.

Getting down on his hands and knees wasn't easy, and nobody else would've tried it if they had a similar wound. But for a situation as dire as this, he merely grumbled as he awkwardly began searching the ground.

Carefully avoiding the blood pools, Jimmy worked from one end of the room to the other. Nothing was easily visible, but that only meant the killer was careful. He already knew that. So, Jimmy looked harder. Under the furniture, the cushions, and the bodies themselves. When that didn't work, he looked even deeper.

Finally, he found something. Hidden inside the pool table was a bank book with deposits and initials; another puzzle he needed to solve, but time was ticking. He couldn't be sure the police weren't already on the way, especially since he had stopped for a nap. After all, they had provided the information that led him there.

Better to finish documenting and searching before trying to decipher the clue he had found. He could always look at it later. Well, unless he was caught.

With that thought spurring him forward, Jimmy quickly stuffed the book into his pocket and looked for anything that might help decode his only clue.

The stink from the 'kitchen' drew him in. Despite the cold, the stench refused to be silenced and left his eyes watering. A few steps in and he found the source of the smell; it came from the trash. Hopefully, that meant it hadn't been emptied, and there was something to be found.

Grimacing, Jimmy got to work, putting his jacket on the counter and rolling up his sleeves. *There goes this pair of gloves. Mo ghrá will kill me, but it cannot be helped.*

A greasy pizza box yielded only cockroaches. They gleefully scurried up to his warmth while he shook them off and sent them swarming to find a new place to shelter.

Despite the sensation of the tiny legs on his skin, Jimmy pressed on. Next was a sandwich wrapper that oozed mayonnaise. Disgusting, but useless. More trash. It stank, it was gross and repulsive, but no new leads.

Almost at the bottom. Rotting orange peels added a disgusting citrus smell, but still nothing. Then, just as he thought he had wasted his time, he suddenly felt something different. He pulled it up very carefully, which brought the stink closer to him. He instinctively raised his hand to cover his nose, but his glove dripped rotten lettuce and stunk just as badly. Gagging, he thrust his glove aside and looked at his prize. At first glance, it was just a wadded-up napkin, covered in ketchup and grease, but he felt something inside.

Carefully, he opened it and revealed its contents—several crumpled sheets of paper that bore ink smudges. Maybe, with work, they'd reveal something. But for now, he felt confident that there was nothing else to find.

After putting the latest clue in his glove for safekeeping, he quickly limped outside, using his jacket to open the knob. He didn't want to leave fingerprints, but there was no way he was putting the gloves back on. They were getting burned as soon as he got a chance, but he didn't have time for that now. Now it was time to make his escape before his luck ran out.

Chapter Five
A Frame Job

JIMMY HURRIED TO THE truck as fast as his aching muscles could go. With Kent already in trouble, he couldn't afford to get caught in a dragnet. After a quick detour to swap out the truck for his car and hide the evidence in Kent's secret compartment, he was off to the hospital. He hadn't seen Kent for himself yet, and despite Doris' ominous warning, he hoped to find his friend well. She always tried to keep him away from danger, and he hoped this was only another way to shield him from Kent's troubles, whatever they might be. Regardless, he needed to see for himself. That was the only way he could be certain, and with a little luck, Kent himself could shed some light on the case.

Jimmy drew his wife into a tender embrace. "Leannán,"

"Aye, so I am, I suppose. You're still chasing Billy's cladhaires; no doubt they'll put you in the ground next to him. I should just enjoy you while I still have you."

"Woman, sure and ye are the most exasperating thing God ever created. I don't know why ye think ye can scare me off when ye know I be about to see him for meself, but ye know I was born with the luck of the Irish. Even if Boss be as bad as ye say, there be no way they'll get me too. I've got one thing he didn't—I know how dirty they'll play. They just caught him off guard, or they never would have gotten to him."

Doris scoffed. "Some luck. I could make a bed of four-leaf clovers for you to sleep in and feed you naught but four-leaf clovers, and you would still be the unluckiest man I know."

He nuzzled her neck and gently kissed the top of her hair. "Now, mo ghrá, ye know that is not true. I have ye, and I have me family, and I have always survived. Sure and I'll be in heaven an hour before the devil even knows I be dead. Why, I even survive daily life with your rugrats, and ye know as well as I do how healthy and wild they be. I've found a family worth more than gold, mo ghrá; certain sure and I'm lucky beyond deserving. And I'll not be letting any cladhaire take that away from me, nor will I let him get away with what he did to me deartháir. It cannot go unanswered, and that ye know it as well as I."

"I know no such thing," Doris insisted, burying her

head in Jimmy's broad chest as she tried to shut out the tired ache that was threatening to overwhelm her.

Jimmy gently cupped her chin. "Get some rest, bean chéile. Ye need it and will be no good to anyone without it. Go on,"

Doris silently refused, and Jimmy finally gave up. He gently pulled her hands to his lips, then limped through the door to check on his friend.

Despite her warning, Jimmy wasn't ready for the sight that awaited him. He shuddered, but moved resolutely to his friend's side and slid over a chair. "Ye look as though ye be trapped in an oubliette. Ye need to find your way back before a banshee comes for ye, Boss."

He paused, hoping for an answer and finally taking the time to take a good look at his friend. Although the detective was feverish and pink, Jimmy couldn't help but smile when he saw the bed. Kent's height was always causing problems, even in the hospital bed, but Lauren had devised an ingenious solution. She had slid a nightstand to the end of the bed, then stacked pillows until he could rest his feet comfortably. It didn't look very sturdy, but at least half his legs weren't dangling awkwardly in the air.

No answer. "Deartháir, ye best get back on your feet

quick. Sure and it be that case ye took that be driving ye nutty, and ye more so for taking it. A Jap? Ye best hope Campbell doesn't find out. There's still so much anger in that one. He's only just warmed up to ye; if he finds ye aiding the enemy, he's liable to regret pulling ye out of that room. So ye must hurry up, ye see, for your own good."

Still silence. "At least ye can point me in the right direction. Who have ye fought with? What did ye not write down?"

There was still no answer, so Jimmy started to leave, gripping his friend's shoulder. "May God give you, for every storm a rainbow, for every tear a smile, for every care a promise, and a blessing in each trial. For every problem life sends, a faithful friend to share, for every sigh a sweet song, and an answer for each prayer."

With that, Jimmy turned to leave. A nagging voice inside him called him back, asking to give his friend more time. One more minute wouldn't hurt anything, so he turned. He was surprised again—although his friend was still disoriented, Kent's bloodshot eyes were open and struggling to focus on him.

"Boss?"

Kent licked his cracked lips, struggling to say something. Jimmy held a cup to his mouth and let him take a long swallow, which earned him a grateful smile from the weary detective. After a few gulps, Jimmy removed the cup and waited patiently while Kent formed his sentence.

"My legs are killing me."

Jimmy chuckled. "Lauren did her best, but ye will feel better in your own bed. What can ye tell me?"

Kent blinked slowly, and Jimmy tried again. "Where are ye, Boss?"

"A hospital?"

"Aye, and do ye know how ye came to be here?"

"Not so much. Break me out?"

"As soon as ye are able, Boss. Me girl be here watching over ye, and yours will be back in a moment. Ye do your part, me boyo, and ye will walk out soon. Ye will be okay, Boss."

Kent shook his head slowly, too confused to be afraid.

"Aye, ye will. Be patient. It'll be okay in the end, but try not to scare the women so. One day Doris will have enough and kill ye herself, and we both know her red hair is no lie. Her Scottish tongue will lay us both flat if ye do not meet her halfway, and I be man enough to admit she scares me. So then, boyo, for everything that be holy, do not tempt me wife to become a murderess."

Kent smiled weakly. "No promises. It'll serve ya right

if you leave me in this place."

"Oh, so ye think ye have it rough? Do ye remember naught of the case ye have saddled me with?"

"The—no. The—not that, maybe?"

"Do ye mean the Jap?"

"Huh?!?"

"Brother, ye take a case and stick me with it. Sure and ye planned it so, didn't ye?"

His brow furrowed as Kent tried to remember. "The Jap—oh! Him. You were never-you weren't supposed to find out."

"Ye knew better than that. I be smarter than ye, so why would ye think ye could hide anything from me? Besides, ye must've picked up a comb on the ground, the way bad luck follows ye around."

Hearing someone at the door, Jimmy turned. It was Lauren, so he said a quick goodbye, then hurried out as fast as his crutches could take him. A goodbye kiss for Doris, some calming words for Mac, and Jimmy made his escape.

The fresh air made him giddy, but a few deep breaths steadied him again. Just because he had never been a prisoner in a hospital didn't mean he liked them any more than Kent did. He had enough bad memories to last a lifetime, and he was happy to be leaving. The antiseptic smell always made his skin crawl, so he took a few extra breaths of the salty sea air to erase the odor from his body before starting toward his car.

He noticed a figure walking toward him and slowed to see who it was. It only took a moment to recognize the man, and Jimmy waved him over. "Sloane!"

"You visiting...your friend?"

"I did, aye. What be ye doing here?"

"I came to do some digging. We found the bodies to match the fingerprints you gave me, and a witness said...your friend..."

"Kent,"

"Kent! Yes. Said Kent ambushed the hooligans, and that's how he got hurt."

"Not possible. Aside from that being completely foreign to Boss' nature, he had already been poisoned. There be no way he could think clearly enough to plan anything. Tell the old bat that be a nice try, but no dice. She's going to have to try harder than that to slander Boss. Besides, if Boss had ambushed anybody, they wouldn't have left alive."

"I know the witness is unreliable and prejudiced. Still, making claims like that when bodies turn up...it needs to get looked at, and more than a few fellas think this could bury him."

"Why do ye stay with such a lousy lot? Ye would make a great addition to our team."

"Then who would save your sorry behinds when you need somebody to run prints? No, I'm fine where I'm at, though thanks for the offer. Aside from some misguided feelings where you fellas are concerned, they're really a good crew. By the way, did you check out the addresses I gave you?"

Jimmy hesitated. Sloane had proven himself an excellent ally over the past year, but he didn't want to put him in an awkward position. If he admitted to finding the bodies and leaving without notifying anyone, that would move him up the suspect list, probably above Kent. There was no way the injured man would dig up leads anytime soon, and who in their right mind would suspect Kent? He had the hospital charts to prove his innocence. And if Jimmy admitted to taking evidence? He would be completely out of luck.

It was settled. Better to ask forgiveness later, if it ever came up. "No, I was knackered and took a nap, then woke up worried about me deartháir. I was on me way to check them out now, but sure and that must be out of the question. I hoped to talk to them, maybe find out who set them on Boss. Maybe if I had gotten there sooner..."

"It probably wouldn't have mattered, anyway. Sorry your lucky break led nowhere."

"I be Irish. Sure and I make me own luck, but I do thank ye for cutting Boss some slack."

Jimmy slid back into his car and sat there, thinking. Where to next? The hospital was a dead end. He felt slightly better about Kent; his friend was, at least, coherent now. But now he was really on the clock. Sloane was going to try his hardest to keep the investigation honest and thorough, but he wouldn't be able to keep his fellow officers off the case for long. His boss would either say he was going soft or too biased to work the case honestly. Then the file would be handed off to somebody who would happily take the easy win. Jimmy couldn't take that chance. Sloane was a good detective, but if he couldn't solve it before they locked Kent up, that would be the end.

A quick check-in with the children, another power nap, then work. He studied the bank book and the files Sloane had given him, looking for a name that matched any of the initials. That yielded a few results, so he began flipping through the phone book. Now, he had the opposite problem. Instead of only a few possibilities, he had dozens. As annoying as that was, at least it would keep him busy.

The afternoon dragged by. Getting background on all his new suspects was tedious, and he hated it. But he was stuck; it wasn't like he could just interview everybody in the city until somebody randomly confessed.

After a while, he tired of dialing numbers and took what he had found to the post office. Several of the names he had collected had moved. That moved them to a different pile—they could still be involved, of course, but it would take longer to check them out and they were less likely to be mixed up in whatever was going on. There were plenty of names right in the city to check out. If they turned out to be innocent, he could always go back and interview the others.

A quick visit to records narrowed it down even more. Several of his names were dead, so even if they were involved in the initial scheme, they had nothing to say that would help solve the murders of the troubled teens. They were moved to a third pile while he kept digging. He couldn't help thinking, *T'would be much easier with a badge. Well, I can find out anything the peelers can. It might take longer, but I can do it better.*

No matter how many ways he looked at it, he felt like he was missing the most important pieces of the puzzle. Sure, it was possible that the Klan had somehow discovered Kent was helping their targets, and their attention to him. It was also possible that he'd wake up and be completely healed the next morning and never use crutches again. It didn't seem likely, though.

Then again, the bitter old woman could have ratted him out as a ne'er-do-well to the wrong person. If so, the visit could be completely unrelated to Masao. That was too big of a coincidence to swallow, and Jimmy decided he had a better chance of waking up and being Cary Grant than for it to be a fluke.

Finally, there were the dead kids themselves. If they were Kent's attackers, there was nothing that pointed to them being in the Klan. Everything he had found said that the only cause they had been loyal to was themselves. The boy's dying words hinted they had been silenced. It didn't make sense...but neither did anything else.

††††††††††††††††††††††††

Jimmy wasn't the only one hitting a dead end. Ever since he had left, Kent had been trying to remember what had landed him in the hospital this time. And the more of his wits he regained, the harder he worked to convince his friends to break him out. Although Mac was sympathetic, he was too timid to agree, and all three women were adamant that he needed to stay conscious for at least two hours before they would even consider it.

After an hour, Kent resigned himself to his hospital bed. Maybe it wouldn't be a complete waste of time. If he could just remember...

Suddenly, the room was dark. His legs ached. He could see the vague outline of a door; at least he wasn't blind. But what had happened to the light?

Maybe stretching would help the tightness in his muscles. He reached out an arm, then stopped. Had his hand just felt skin?

He turned his head slowly. There was no point in bothering whoever was lying there when all he wanted was to identify them. Besides, his stomach lurched every time he moved; maybe moving slower would help.

Kent laid back on his pillow for a moment, closing his eyes so they could adjust. When he opened them again, the first thing he saw was Doris, sprawled in a chair in the corner, snoring. How much time had he lost? Where had the sun gone?

Something—or some**one**—shifted, snatching him back to the present. A familiar scent floated by. Lauren. So that's what the pressure on his chest was. He smiled at her, then started thinking again. Who else had come?

He was trying to remember. He thought Lieutenant Sloane had stopped by, but he wasn't sure. What he was sure of was that he had spoken to Jimmy. It seemed like his room stayed crowded, but he remembered a private conversation with Lauren.

Or did he? It was so frustrating. The memories all contradicted each other, each one similar, yet all so different. And despite those differences, they all seemed to be one. And what was even more frustrating was that, if his memory wasn't playing a cruel trick on him, Jimmy was every bit as clueless as he was.

No matter what he was thinking about, one thought kept nagging at him. What good was a detective who couldn't remember his own clues?

Although he didn't like it, that question had a simple answer. A detective without clues was useless. He might as well quit and get a job as a soda jerk. But crowds terrified him, so that was no good either. Somehow, he had to remember, no matter how difficult it was. But then, how could it be easy when he didn't even know what he needed to remember?

After pondering his dilemma for a few moments, he remembered something about poison. Yes, Jimmy said somebody had poisoned him. Wait, poisoned who? Had Jimmy been poisoned?

Kent's stomach churned again. No, he had been poisoned. The way he felt was evidence enough of that. But who had poisoned him? He couldn't remember if he had any visitors at all, friendly or otherwise. He couldn't even remember going home. But he remembered Chad coming home early. Did he know who had visited? No. Jimmy would have already asked him.

Kent balled his fist in frustration, his entire arm tensing as he forgot Lauren's dainty hand resting gently on him. She jumped up in surprise, wiping the sleep out of her eyes as she sleepily focused on Kent.

"William? What is the matter?"

"Nothin', darlin'. Just aggravated. Don't suppose you'd be interested in springing me now?"

"No, William. Not yet. You just lost seven hours. I told you, you need to stay awake for two hours minimum before we even tried to get you released."

"Lars, I ain't waitin' two hours. I'm gettin' outta here while I still can. I'm steady, scout's honor, but I'm not stayin' here any longer."

"But—"

"NO! I am going <u>home</u>."

Kent was too animated in his response and forgot to whisper. Doris tumbled out of her chair and Mac came charging into the room, looking for danger.

"Sorry, y'all, just little ol' me," Kent smiled sheepishly.

"Aye, I can see that. What are you doing?"

"Well, Kitten, I was just telling Lauren here thanks for the hotel suite and room service, but I'm homeward bound."

"And you're glaikit enough to mean that, too." Doris snorted.

"Yes'm I am. You're the best nurse in this place, and you've doctored me back from worse scrapes than this."

Doris scoffed, causing Kent to pull her in for a brotherly squeeze before weakly tousling her hair. "Reckon you need your own bed just as much as I do. Why, Jimmy'd never even recognize that mop—and what do you think Myrna would say?"

The name caused Doris to stiffen; she wasn't sure how she felt about having her younger sister back in her life yet. Too late she realized Kent had successfully distracted her long enough to be on his feet. "William Edward Kent, you best get back in that bed, or I'll nae be responsible for you!"

"Help me bust out, and I'll stay in bed for a week if you say so. I'll even watch the kids while you and Jimmy go out on a date."

"You are impossible. Well, do nae just stand there,

Samuel McDonald. Get his clothes. Lauren, be a good lass and fetch the doctor before this giant eejit topples over and knocks us all down. I swear, Billy, you're as big a fool as you are a man, and that's saying something."

"Aww, Kitten, you know ya love me."

"Phooey!"

†††††††††††††††††††††††††

It took the rest of the night, but Kent finally got his discharge, much to the chagrin of the hospital staff. By the time the first ray from the morning sun brushed the earth below, Lauren was helping Kent out of her car and into her home. He protested one last time, but she remained steadfast, refusing to budge no matter how much he insisted he was ready to go to his home. "Chad hasn't finished getting it ready yet, and you're not ready to be alone."

Mrs. Williams met them at the front door. "How are you feeling, Mr. Kent? You don't look at all well, though I have seen you worse. Not by much, mind you, but I have. Why aren't you in the hospital?"

Lauren was out of breath from supporting him, but took the time to give him a smug smile. He ignored it. "I'll be right as rain in a day or so, you'll see. I'm already a thousand percent better, but Lars insists I need a babysitter."

His laughing eyes looked so pained, his tone so indignant, pleading so desperately for understanding, that Lauren almost felt guilty. Almost. "Not a babysitter, William. A nurse. You would do the same for me."

Her gentle tone brought a resigned expression to his face, and he smiled tenderly at her. He still couldn't resist needling her. "Yeah. The difference is, you'd need it."

She huffed and stiffened, while Mrs. Williams laughed softly. "I'm very pleased to see you in such good spirits, Mr. Kent, but Mr. Campbell and I are still cleaning your room, and the chemicals would not help your condition at all. Besides, what if those ruffians should return before you are fully recovered? Mr. Campbell is watching your home, but he does not need the added worry of keeping you safe. Trust me, Mr. Kent. No one thinks you need a babysitter."

Mrs. Williams paused and leaned in conspiratorially. "Lauren does worry about you so. If something so trivial makes her feel useful, then isn't it worth it? It is not as though we do not have room in this lonely old house, and this place still gives us the shivers sometimes. I warrant we will both sleep better having you here."

Kent mumbled, but she had convinced him. He

offered no more complaints, and they soon had him in his custom bed, stretched out comfortably. "All right, I've been good. Now can I get my notes, please?"

"You are impossible." Despite rolling her eyes, Lauren gave him the phone and patiently waited as he dialed Jimmy.

†††††††††††††††††††††††††††

THIRTY MINUTES LATER, JIMMY handed Kent the files, then watched him for any glimmer of recognition. Both men hoped that something within the photographs would trigger a memory, maybe even reveal the identity of the poisoner. At the very least, the identity of Kent's female guest could shed some light on a case that seemed to exist only in shadows, and perhaps even reveal a motive for the attacks. Anything was better than what they had now.

Both detectives were disappointed. Kent studied the photos closely, but couldn't remember any more than he had before.

Exasperated, Kent's shoulders slumped dejectedly. "What now?"

Jimmy shrugged. "I will keep working, Boss. Certain sure and ye can take that to the bank. T'would have been easier if ye could give me something, but there be no fun in easy. Lucky for ye, I'm on the job. Seeing as I'm the smart one, we'll get this solved pronto."

He playfully punched Kent's shoulder before limping toward the door. "Ye look at those as much as ye like, but listen to your little Florence Nightingale. Do not be pushing yourself too hard. I can manage without ye a few days. Make the most of your little 'vacation'."

He left, and his friend collapsed back onto the pillow. Kent couldn't understand why he was so exhausted, but he didn't have the strength to look at the files anymore. He wasn't even strong enough to move them to the nightstand. But when he caught a whiff of Chanel No. 5 and heard Lauren's light step, he forced open an eye. "What are you doing New Year's Eve?"

Although he hoped his crooning would sound like Sinatra, his voice was still raspy. All he could muster was Durante, and Lauren giggled before handing him some water. "If your voice is any indication, I'll be right here, keeping your water pitcher full."

"I mean it, Lars,"

The playful tone in his voice was gone, and his tired eyes searched hers earnestly while pleading for an answer. He had completely caught her off guard, but she still wondered if she was reading too much into his new attitude. She had never seen him so sincere before...

Lauren clasped his hand. "Whatever I am doing, it will be with you. I promised, remember?"

Kent sighed as he began drifting off to the first peaceful sleep he could remember. There were plenty of dreams he'd discovered existed only in his mind, but he was glad to know that he hadn't imagined this one. Partly because it meant he hadn't hallucinated the whole thing, and partly because it meant he wasn't crazy. But mostly because it meant that she wanted to start seeing him.

If he was being completely honest with himself, he was glad that she was so eager to begin the new year with him. Her manners and thoughtfulness had impressed him the first time they met, and that had only deepened the more he got to know her.

As he had become more acquainted with her, he had been surprised at how strong and determined she was. Shockingly, she was as protective of her friends as he was, and although she seemed meek as a lamb, the instant her friends were threatened, she became a tigress. She was smart, young, with her whole life in front of her, and she wanted to spend time with him. He couldn't imagine why, but she did. Sure, at first he had found excuses to see her, wanting to reassure her that despite her past, not everybody was evil. Later, he had brought Jimmy along to help fix up her dilapidated old house, using him as a chaperone, but the two were comfortable together.

For somebody with as much baggage as William Kent, that was everything. And for the first time in years, he didn't dread going to sleep.

††††††††††††††††††††††††††

WHEN HE LEFT LAUREN'S house, Jimmy felt the weight of the world crushing him. He had put on a brave face for Kent, but with nobody watching, he didn't have to pretend anymore. Promising somebody confined to their bed results was one thing. It was easy. Delivering on that promise? That was something else entirely. He hadn't told Kent about the latest development yet. What good would it do to worry him more? If the pictures hadn't jarred his memory, finding out he was suspected of murdering eight people certainly wouldn't. And Kent was still too weak to help figure out who was behind the frame job. The only thing he could help with was providing the missing details of that night—nothing earth-shattering, but anything at all would've been useful.

Yet his friend couldn't even do that. And as much as Jimmy sympathized with his friend, letting him worry himself to death wouldn't help anybody. Yes, he remembered what it was like to feel helpless, to know that everybody else knew something you'd never remember. He also remembered how far it would push you to prove that it didn't define you, that you were still a man.

Giving Kent another reason to feel like he had something to prove was a bad idea. The police might come knocking at any moment and haul Kent away in handcuffs.

Well, that wasn't going to happen. Not if Jimmy had anything to say about it. Kent was the most decent person he had ever met, and there was no way he would let his friend be executed for doing the right thing.

He finally decided to question Kent's client again. Things had been moving fast for the detective. Who was to say that the same problems weren't plaguing the man who had dragged Kent into this mess?

The drive was agonizing. He had the address but wasn't looking forward to the interview, so he wanted to drag it out as much as possible. The best way to do that was to drive slowly, and he was. Other drivers honked furiously until they could pass him, but there was no force on earth strong enough to compel him to speed up.

Despite having driven at a snail's pace, he eventually

arrived at his destination and switched off Kent's truck, but almost left again. Kent had described a neat, tidy little home with an immaculate yard. This place was a mess. But it was the right address, so he decided to knock on the door.

The closer he got to the house, the worse it looked. The landscaping had been destroyed, and not even the mailbox had been spared. It was thrust through the car's windshield, crushed and splintered, sporting a lone red dot. Another was painted on the car itself, while a third covered the entire front wall of the house. "Subtle lot," Jimmy mumbled, kicking at the charred remnants of a cross. He gingerly made his way through the remnants of an Azalea, his eyes studying the house's broken windows. The thugs were thorough; the shutters hung haphazardly from their hinges, making an eerie creaking, clanking sound in the night.

Another cross. That didn't fit, but neither did anything else in this case. As he walked past it, he couldn't help himself. "Praise the Lord, and pass the ammunition—we're all between perdition and the deep blue sea."

He steeled himself as he prepared to knock on the door. This was the moment he'd been dreading, and there was no way to put it off now. Besides, Kent's client could be on the other side of the door, bleeding to death.

After a deep breath, he pounded loudly on the remnants of what had once been a proud oak door. "Oi! Anybody here?"

There was a slight shuffling sound before the door creaked open. Both men sighed in relief after recognizing the other.

"I am most relieved it is only you," Masao said, showing Jimmy inside before shuffling toward the tattered remains of his couch. "For just a moment, I thought that perhaps the cowards who had destroyed my home came back to finish their work. How is Detective-san?"

"He'll live. They don't come any tougher than Boss. I wanted to ask ye some questions, if that be all right."

"Hai."

"When did this all start?"

"As I told Detective-san, it began two months ago."

"And how long have ye lived here?"

"I tell all this to your employer already. We moved here in 1945, soon after the bombs were dropped on my home." Although his eyes grew misty remembering the fiery sight, Masao's face remained expressionless.

For a moment, Jimmy felt sorry for him. The moment passed quickly, though; it passed as soon as he remembered the camp where Kent had been held. Most of that day remained a blur, even after fourteen years; lost to time and the shot to the head. Still, he remembered enough to harbor a deep resentment on behalf of his friend.

"Well, if ye have been living here so long, why would they be after ye now?"

"That is very good question, and one I have been asking myself. I do not know what could cause such an interest in my community."

Jimmy began double-checking the notes he already had, as Masao again related the events that had caused the residents to live in fear. His neighbors had been tormented until, one by one, they had all fled. Why they were suddenly being exterminated was anybody's guess, but there was a pattern to each attack.

The first warning was a rose. The family was given a week, then a cross was burned in the yard. Another week passed, and then the father would be beaten. After that, the house was trashed, and another cross burned.

They seemed to be on a rotating schedule. The first family would get a rose. During the following week, a second family would receive the ominous flower.

Aside from him, only the very first family had held on after receiving the first warning, and they had paid with their lives. Once the other neighbors discovered what came next, they chose survival over property.

The victims all shared Japanese ancestry, but had lived their lives in America for different periods. Some had been there for their entire lives, even before the war, while others had only lived there a few months. They worked in different fields and lived different lives; some had fought to maintain the traditions of their ancestral home, while others had embraced the culture of their adopted homeland.

Again, Jimmy felt a pang of sympathy for the man. The matter-of-fact way that he spoke of intimidation was all too familiar, and the allure of blending in to avoid being singled out hit home. Many times, when he was younger, he had practiced talking like his classmates, hoping to avoid a beating. He always ended up getting one, anyway; his accent was too thick. That had driven him to boxing, and he had never again tried to hide his identity. Instead, he had become fiercely proud of his heritage and a champion featherweight.

But wasn't that different? He had done nothing to warrant the hatred hurled at him. And he certainly wasn't related to anyone responsible for the Second World War and the loss of millions of lives. However misguided these thugs were, they had a reason to be

A FRAME JOB

wary of the enemy in their midst.

Except they didn't. This was a quiet community, most of whom had no ties to the Imperials who had caused so much pain. The only one connected to that group was sitting in front of him, battered but still proud. Nobody besides his wife knew his background, and even if he had been the reason for the attacks, why had everybody else been driven off first? Besides, the dead kids had no link to the war. That argument made no sense; they had no reason to target anyone without money or power. Yet despite some victims being wealthy, their valuables had been destroyed, not stolen. It just didn't make sense.

Chapter Six
The Laughing Flames

J IMMY SAT THERE, LOST in thought for several minutes before realizing that the room was silent. He glanced up and studied his companion; Masao was visibly exhausted and suffering from the beatings he had endured. "Do ye have anywhere else where ye can get some rest? Maybe with your bhean chéile—wife?"

"No. I will not be shamed by such dishonorable men."

"What of your wife?"

"She took my children to safety almost two days ago." Masao was visibly pained, despite his best efforts to conceal his emotions. "It is for the best that she is not here. She is so afraid now, even without suffering the indignities that have plagued me. Had she remained, she may have done something foolish and brought dishonor upon us. It is my duty to protect my family. To my great shame, I could not do so alone and was forced to hire your employer. I have most regretfully put him in the same predicament which I find myself in."

"Your wife left ye knowing ye were in such bad shape?"

As soon as he said it, Jimmy wished he could take the words back. He wasn't trying to be rude. He was doing everything he could to hide the surprise and disgust in his voice. But the thought of a wife leaving her husband so badly injured was something he couldn't fathom. Maybe Doris had spoiled him; her Scottish pride would never allow her to abandon him, and she loved him too much to leave him to face death alone. They had fought about that for as long as they had known each other. Even her motherly instinct wasn't enough to force her to betray him. She would send her children to her mother's at the first sign of danger, but nothing could convince her to go with them.

Still, Jimmy tried to remind himself that everyone wasn't as strong as his wife, and even she had left once. Granted, it had taken Kent some work to convince her to leave, but he had. She had taken their kids and ran, waiting for him to find Jimmy.

Maybe he was being too hard on the woman. He hadn't met her, but she seemed to put her children first, and he couldn't blame her for that. Leaving her husband in such a vulnerable state seemed calloused, but what if she had stayed? The whole family could be dead. Instead, Masao had only been beaten—badly, it was true—but he was alive, and so were they.

If Masao heard the note of disdain, he hid it well. His expression remained unchanged, but he seemed so frail that Jimmy debated offering him help. In the end, he decided against it. Masao had two things left; his honor and his pride. There was no way Jimmy was going to rob him of that.

After watching him for a few minutes more, Jimmy asked permission to search the house. Maybe, just maybe, there would be something to explain the intrusion. If he got really lucky, there might be something there to identify the men behind the latest attack. He wouldn't find anything out from Masao; it seemed like he remembered about as much from his attack as Kent did. But no matter how important those questions were, they weren't the most pressing ones. Jimmy wanted nothing more than to answer the youth's dying question: 'Why?'

Why. That summed up his dilemma nicely. With Masao's blessing, he secured the house. It wasn't large, but the destruction was thorough. Jimmy knew it would be a stroke of luck to find anything in the mess, but he doggedly continued his search.

He hoped to learn more about who had done this to Masao's house, but no such luck. The man couldn't tell him much; he had been ambushed sometime after returning from Kent's house. He was unconscious for most of it, and he couldn't remember the rest. All he knew was that when he woke up, his house was a wreck. Unlike Kent's house, there were no signs of fire.

Hopefully, in time, Masao would remember what had happened. But Jimmy didn't have time. Besides, with those head wounds, it was just as likely that the memory would be of something completely unrelated. Anything the man said shouldn't be trusted.

At least this second attack meant a chance to uncover the mastermind. The thugs were dead, so they couldn't have done it. That meant there was a second group of attackers. He had identified the kids; he could figure out who was behind this attack, too. And once he did, he could eventually find the crook in charge.

So, he searched. Every slashed rug, every broken vase, every shredded sheet was examined, but they refused to help him.

Never one to quit, Jimmy kept searching. He found some strands of cashmere; this group was definitely better dressed than the youths had been.

Although he kept searching, Jimmy couldn't find anything else useful. That didn't matter: although he wanted to go home more than anything else, he couldn't. One look at Masao told him that the man shouldn't be left alone. So, he called Doris, told her not to wait up, and then settled in for the night, knowing one of two things was about to happen. Either nothing would happen and he could get some rest, or there would be a third attack. He preferred the second choice, but Masao didn't look like he'd survive a third round. Having seen pictures of the man's family—especially the impish little girl who reminded him so much of his own daughter—he decided to do everything possible to keep him alive.

Jimmy positioned a chair in the corner of Suki's bedroom so that he could watch the window and the door. He wasn't going to sleep—too risky. But he'd only slept a few hours in the truck, and not at all the night before. Two days with only three hours of sleep was a lot harder to manage than it was before he had kids. But he couldn't fall asleep—it wasn't safe. He couldn't afford to close his eyes; there was no backup. Still, he couldn't help it. The chair was too much temptation; he fell asleep instantly.

†††††††††††††††††††††††††††

THE ROOM WAS SO hot it seemed like all the air had been sucked out of it. Jimmy woke slowly, his eyes burning. Smoke filled the room, making it hard to breathe. He had lived this nightmare before. But was he sleeping? It felt so real, so much like that day back in '37. And although that fire had almost cost him his life, it was also the thing that chipped through Doris' icy exterior enough to give him a chance. Cars backfiring, balloons popping, and planes flying overhead bothered him. Fire never had. No. This was real, and he needed to move.

As he walked down the hall, he heard nothing. Then a sound, blending perfectly with the crackling flames—was someone laughing? He ignored the pain in his back and the heat trying to fuse his skin to the crutches as he crept forward, ignoring the smoldering embers dancing around his head.

Masao was slumped on the couch. On the floor by his feet was an empty bottle of Jack Daniels, and a man was standing over him, a triumphant smirk on his face. In his hands, the intruder held a kyu gunto, which he was about to thrust through the unconscious man; the flames dancing on the wall bathed the man's face in an evil glow.

Jimmy had seen enough. He lunged forward, forgetting his pain as he closed the space between them, using his crutches to vault across the room in a long leap. Nothing else mattered; he had to get to his prey before the coward could finish his job.

Within seconds, Jimmy was nearly on the intruder. He had gotten within a few feet of the man when the would-be assassin pivoted, slicing the long blade skillfully through the air. Jimmy blocked with his left crutch, neatly catching the blade in the metal frame and twisting it.

As the man hurried to catch his balance, Jimmy regained his own footing. The man shoved Jimmy back into the flaming wall, and Jimmy grabbed a fiery drape to keep from falling. That gave him a second as the intruder closed in. Jimmy pushed the button on his crutch, a blade flipped out instantly, and Jimmy lunged for the man. As the thug dodged the blade, he ducked into Jimmy's merciless right hook.

That was enough to daze the would-be killer. He paused to shake his head, to clear it—only a moment, but that was all Jimmy needed. The detective saw his opening and took it, thrusting his hand into the man's throat, sending the goon staggering backward, gasping for air from the punch he never saw coming.

Jimmy didn't stop to see if the man was dead or not. He yanked out the thug's wallet to identify the man later. If he had time to come back after getting Kent's client out safely, then, and only then, would he worry about saving the trash on the floor. He certainly wouldn't lose any sleep over it if he couldn't.

"Nagasaki, get up!" Jimmy barked. No response. There wasn't time to check for a pulse now; the flames were licking at his feet. He propped Masao on his crutches and stood behind him, holding him up as he awkwardly hurried them both outside.

With Masao safely out of harm's way, Jimmy turned to go back for the other man. The white-hot flames urged him back, but he ignored the blistering heat and pushed on.

Before he could get through the door, the roof of the house collapsed. Although the man inside was now silent, the laughing flames mocked his failure.

With nothing left to do for the arsonist, Jimmy limped back to Masao. He felt for a pulse, then sighed in relief. The pulse was weak but steady, and the man's chest was rising in shallow, almost imperceptible breaths.

As Jimmy sat the man up and gave him some ipecac syrup from the medicine bag in his car, he monitored the burning house. It had gone up so fast! Well, that was why he used asbestos for both his house and Kent's.

Because of that one difference, the Nagasaki house had become a blazing inferno, and Kent's hadn't.

Yet even without being fireproofed, Masao's home shouldn't have burned so quickly. He would have to come back after the flames died and investigate.

While he waited for the ipecac to work, he checked Masao for any other injuries. He was clearly suffering from alcohol poisoning, but Jimmy needed to be certain there was nothing else. After all, Masao wouldn't have just sat there silently and waited for the man to drown him in alcohol. From what Jimmy had seen when he searched the house, Masao only had saké, and it appeared to be only for special occasions. That meant the bottle of Jack by the couch was a plant.

Jimmy finished checking the man. No additional injuries. When and if Masao woke up, maybe he could explain what had happened. Right now, Jimmy just wanted to keep the man alive.

Masao began gagging, and Jimmy held him up so he wouldn't choke. He knew all of Doris' tricks and was using as many as he could to help the injured man.

Still, he knew it wasn't enough. He needed to get Masao to a hospital before it was too late. It was going to be tricky to get Masao up from the ground, but he didn't want to drag the man, either. He pulled his truck as close as possible, then began heaving Masao toward it. Although grateful that the man was only 5'4"—about the same height as Doris—he was still dead weight, and Jimmy was exhausted from the fight. Thank goodness his slight build made him easier to maneuver than Kent!

It took longer than Jimmy wanted, but he eventually got Masao into the cab and peeled off toward the hospital. Although Jimmy wasn't fond of the man, he still felt responsible for his safety. Thankfully, the roads were practically deserted at 3 a.m., and less traffic meant fewer obstacles. Good. It also meant less chance of blending in if somebody had been watching the Nagasaki house for survivors. Decidedly less good, but not bad enough to keep Jimmy from flattening the accelerator to the floor.

Soon they were at the hospital, and Jimmy was once again maneuvering the unconscious Masao onto his crutches. A few moments later, and he was beating on the door for admittance. "Oi! You in there, open up. I've got an injured man out here."

Several orderlies scurried out and transferred Masao to a stretcher, with Jimmy limping along behind. *Begorrah, but I be shattered, certain sure. Best get this over with and get to me own bed, I'm getting too old for this, and 'tis finally all catching up with me.*

He couldn't tell the nurse much, but he told her everything he knew. Knowing he couldn't help the man any more, he called Sloane—first at work, then at home.

A sleepy voice answered on the sixth ring. "Hello?"

"Sloane, this be Jimmy O'Sullivan—Irish. I need ye here at the hospital yesterday."

Although Sloane was still grumbling when he hung up, he was standing in front of Jimmy less than ten minutes later. "All right...Irish, what gives?"

"I'm here with Boss's client, a Jap. Boss kept it quiet, and I'd appreciate it if you did too, but it's the reason the 'Klan' visited him." Jimmy figured this information wouldn't be enough to put a target on Sloane, but would hopefully be sufficient for the policeman to do his job without getting in Jimmy's way. "After they beagnach maraíodh him a few days ago, I picked his case up and have been chasing his banshees ever since. I was at the client's house, and he was attacked again about an hour ago. I put him down and got me client out, but the fire was too hot—"

"Fire?"

"Did I forget that? Sure and he was trying to stage the murder as a suicide. Begorrah, it's cold in here. Me client said his community is being held hostage, and I wanted...oh, saints preserve us...Doris..."

Jimmy blinked, trying to focus as his mouth formed words without sound. "Doris."

Sloane caught him as he slumped to the ground, calling for help. As Jimmy was placed on a gurney, the police detective noticed the crimson under his jacket for the first time. "Well, Irish, you're one tough nut to crack. I'll call your wife for ya, if I can just remember her name."

He thumbed through Jimmy's wallet until he found her name on an old letter—yellowed with age, singed, and blood-stained, but still legible. He tried their home first but got no answer. Remembering that Doris' mother always watched the kids, he looked at the letter again to find her maiden name.

There it was. Petrie. Well, there shouldn't be too many of those.

Except there were.

Twelve Petries later, he finally found the right one and summoned Mrs. O'Sullivan, who wasted no time charging into the room. "Where is mo ghaol, mo chridhe?"

Before the nurse could answer, Sloane pulled her aside. Unfortunately for him, she was not in the mood for questions. "Now see here, you can nae keep me from an duine agam, and if you try, t'will be the last you ever do."

Sloane let go of her arm and stepped back. He had only seen her temper once, but that was enough to let him know he did not want to be on her bad side. "I would never dream of trying, ma'am. I only wanted to let you know that he's not out of surgery yet."

Her voice raised an octave as she glared at him. "And why would mo ghràidh need surgery?"

"It—it looks like something slashed him." The policeman wasn't easily intimidated, but she had him sweating profusely and floundering to give her an answer. His explanation was brief and answered almost nothing, but it was the best he could come up with under her scathing gaze.

"Something? Oh, aye, that helps. It answers every question I have. I need nae stay here, as you know it all already, and clearly have everything under control."

"Ma'am, I'm sorry—"

"Aye, that be true enough! Why can ye nae be helpful?"

Out of the corner of his eye, Sloane glimpsed Kent walking through the door. He looked pleadingly at his friend; he might not understand how to deal with Doris, but surely Kent did by now.

Seeing the panicked look on Sloane's face, Kent grinned before shuffling weakly toward them, his confident swagger a victim of his brush with death. Although he wasn't holding onto walls for support anymore, he wasn't confident enough to venture too far away from one, just in case.

Doris was still scolding Sloane when Kent finally made it to them. He silently wrapped his arms around her, engulfing her even as she fussed through his jacket. "Kitten, he'll be fine."

"Oh, I have nae a doubt about that. The pair of you are only working together to drive me to an early grave; there is nae a chance that stubborn Irish blood would let him quit before he succeeds."

Kent grinned and squeezed her in a bear hug, but she pushed him away and sent him staggering into the nurse's desk. "Kitten, it's okay. If killing me makes you happy—"

"Argh! William Kent, you are an incorrigible, aggravating, stubborn..."

"Charming, thoughtful, caring..."

"Oooh! You-you-you..."

Kent patted her arm as she helped steady him before giving his best imitation of Jimmy. "Aye, 'tis me and no one but."

Sloane couldn't believe how quickly Kent had calmed her down, or that anything he'd said worked. If he had ever talked to a woman like that, Sloane was confident she would have decked him.

Well, the crisis had been averted, so it was time to get some answers. It was best to be careful, though; after all, Jimmy had said the case was secret. "Any idea what he was up to?"

"Honestly, no. I barely know what I was up to, but he should fill us in when he gets out of surgery. Your turn. What do ya know?"

Sloane groaned inwardly as he tried to figure out another non-answer, but Doris dismissed him with a wave of her hand. "You are wasting your time if you think you'll be getting an answer out of him. He knows nothing."

Although Sloane thought he was getting away without an answer, Kent had been studying him. Even when he was managing Doris, he had never looked away. He knew there was more that Sloane wasn't saying. They had known each other long enough for Kent to recognize his bluffs, and Sloane was doing them all—shuffling, holding eye contact too long, and intercepting each conversation with questions before anybody could ask him one. Doris hadn't tried to murder him, so she must not know about Masao. Besides, Jimmy wouldn't have driven himself to a hospital. He was married to an excellent nurse. But he would have brought someone there that he wanted to be kept secret. Could his client be there, too? As soon as Doris was gone, he'd ask, but at the moment, he was worried about Jimmy, and a nurse was headed toward them.

"Mrs. O'Sullivan? He'll be out in a moment. He lost a lot of blood, but the doctor is confident that he'll be just fine. No lifting anything, though."

Doris chuckled with relief. "Well, Billy boy, looks like you'll be carrying your own weight from now on."

The nurse looked puzzled, but continued. "And no physical exertion."

Sloane had a question of his own. "Can you tell me what happened?"

"The doctor said it looked like the burns on him will hurt, but they'll all heal. None of them required more than ointment and bandages. But the gash to his chest caused the trouble, and if he isn't careful, he could tear the stitches open again. Here comes Mr. O'Sullivan now."

Doris followed her husband into his room, but the nurse was back almost instantly. "I don't want to disturb them so soon, but I forgot to return her husband's wallet and other personal effects."

"I'll see that she gets this," Kent volunteered.

When the nurse left, Kent commented, "This ain't his. Why do I get the feelin' you might know who it belongs to?"

"Maybe because I might. I'm not sure, mind you, but Ir...Jimmy said he fought with somebody, but he couldn't get the guy out before your client's house burned down. Do you think it could belong to the dead man? Would he pick a man's pocket before leaving him to die?"

"First, he wouldn't leave anybody to croak unless he had no choice. The fact he got burned oughta testify to that. Second, Jimmy never misses a clue. If he thought he needed to preserve evidence, then yeah, he'd do whatever was necessary. How about you tell me everything you know?"

"There's not much to tell. Irish didn't have much time to tell me anything, and I don't think he wanted to say much, anyway. Now, you tell me what you know."

"One more question. Is Nagasaki in there?"

"Your client? A Japanese fella?"

"Yup."

"Yeah, Irish brought him in. The doctor said he'd been

drugged and is suffering from some serious alcohol poisoning, but the doc said somebody—probably Irish—had given him Ipecac, and he's through the worst of it now. Aside from a killer hangover, he'll be okay."

"What about his family?"

Sloane jerked his head up to meet Kent's gaze. This was new information. "What family?"

"He's got a wife and three kids. The boys were quiet, but she's swell."

"Irish didn't mention a family."

"Well, he might not've had a chance. He's really been behind the eight-ball with this one. He didn't know anything 'til he took over for me, and all I can tell him about it is what I've read. I can't remember anything from the past two, maybe three, days.

"If you'll excuse me a minute, I am 'shattered', as Jimmy would say. I need to sit down before I fall over, and I might as well visit my client while I'm at it. Imagine he could use the company, and it might knock something loose in this ornery noggin of mine,"

"You're gonna have to tell me what happened sometime, and it'd be better if you did it when it was just the two of us."

"Now, Sloane, even your buddies can't think I

poisoned myself. I'll be back. I'm just going in that room, right there, that has my client in it. Cross my heart, I won't jump—or climb—outta any windows. Even if I did, I don't think I could outrun you right now."

Kent talked to Masao for a few minutes, but soon tired of the one-sided conversation. There were more important ways he could spend his time, so he left. To his surprise, four officers were standing with Sloane. One particularly surly one smirked at him. "You Will Kent?"

"William, and yeah. What's going on?"

"You're coming in for questioning is what's going on. We want to know about the eight kids you killed."

His jaw dropped. Eight kids? Kent couldn't believe it. "I did what now?"

Lauren walked through the door just in time to see a man shoving Kent toward the door. It was rough, but wouldn't have been enough to make him stumble if it weren't for the poison. As it was, it sent him spinning into the desk.

Her face flushed with rage, Lauren didn't wait to find out anything else. She bolted to her friend and shoved the laughing officer out of her way, 'accidentally' driving her heel into his shoe.

The man's face was livid as he snatched her up. It

wasn't enough to make Lauren back down; she only smirked at him. "Oh, did I do that? I am so sorry. I can be such a klutz, but you know that."

The man's face reddened as he realized she was making fun of his inability to solve her case nearly two years before. "You were crazy then, and you're crazy now."

Kent lunged at the man, but Sloane stepped between them. "Lazlo, cut it out. This is not the time to be a schoolyard bully."

The officer sputtered with rage. "You're standing up for that—that..."

A second voice chimed in. "Come on, Ted, you went too far."

Realizing he was alone as the horrified nurse rushed to Lauren's side, he stepped back, sulking. "I'm just doing my job—they resisted, and she assaulted me."

His buddies burst out laughing. "Oh yeah, you were lucky to get away alive."

The nurse had moved from Lauren to Kent, recognizing him from his brief stay the day before. "He won't answer any questions today. He's not strong enough."

Lauren paled and ran to the bathroom, leaving everyone except Kent staring after her in confusion.

"Tummy trouble. She's been having it all day; it's the only way I could sneak out to come check on my brother."

A few minutes later, Lauren dragged herself out of the bathroom. Kent discreetly dabbed the corner of her mouth. "You okay?"

She nodded. "Can we go home now, William? Please?"

Kent looked at Sloane for an answer.

"Sure, just don't leave town."

The pair left him arguing with the other four men and headed to Kent's truck, leaving Lauren's car for later. "You up for some sleuthing?"

"But-what-why-fine."

Kent patted her arm sympathetically. "I can drop you first if you'd rather."

An indignant expression covered Lauren's face. "What kind of damsel in distress do you think I am? My stomach is unsettled because you have run me ragged. I am not an invalid, although you may have to clean your truck."

Kent opened the door, leaning back for some fresh air, then noticed the bloodstains on the driver's seat. "I'm going to have to do that anyway. Driving around sitting on Jimmy's blood is unnerving, even for me."

"Might I inquire where we're going?"

"Nagasaki's house. Jimmy didn't add notes last night, but before that, he added Nagasaki was the latest in a long line of hate crimes. Seems like I heard that before, but I can't remember why for love nor money."

Masao's house was still smoldering. A few charred walls remained; Lauren stared at it, a mixed expression of fear, anger, guilt, and awe on her face. "If it weren't for Chad, this would be your house."

Kent nodded grimly. "Thank God for small favors. Course, Jimmy did use asbestos siding on my house, so maybe it wasn't such a miracle.

"I doubt we'll learn much, but let's get to it."

The pair split up. Lauren searched for clues in the mess of sand left behind by the firemen and police, although finding anything seemed like an impossible task.

Kent's job was equally daunting, although he didn't waste time thinking about it. For the first time, he was grateful for the cold; the thirty-degree chill had cooled the smoldering ruins to a more bearable temperature. They were still miserably hot, but he could manage it. After all, he had survived one fire as a child, and another, years later, on the sinking hell ship. This was nothing compared to either of those.

He quickly locked the thoughts away. He knew that if he didn't focus, the memories would drown him. What had Jimmy called it? An oubliette? He'd have to look that up, but it sounded like an appropriate description of what was happening to him.

As Kent moved closer, he smelled it. A stomach-churning variation on barbeque. The smell of burned human flesh was unmistakable and made burying his memories so much harder.

"William?"

Kent shook his head and looked up to see Lauren standing just outside the charred remains of the door frame, looking worriedly at him. "Yeah, Lars?"

"I've been calling you for five minutes. Are you all right?"

"I'm fine."

He didn't mean it to sound as harsh as it did, but he hoped that would be enough to keep her from asking anything else, even as he wiped the beads of sweat from his forehead with a shaking hand.

Seeing the hurt on her face, he spoke gently. "I'm aces, Lars. Just a little warm."

Her face plainly showed her disbelief, but she started working again, leaving him to the unpleasant task of searching for the body—or at least where it had been before being whisked away to the morgue.

Given the devastation, he didn't expect that to be easy, but it was even harder than he expected. A small section of the wall remained near the door, the only section that was relatively undamaged. The body had sheltered it, and the body must have belonged to the wallet now in his pocket. Good thing Sloane had let him leave; if the other cops had caught him with it, they'd probably charge him with this, too.

Still, he needed to find answers to the tough questions, or Jimmy would end up in the cell next to him. After all, Jimmy's good nature went only so far, and given the hostile attitude of the cops he had just faced, any conversation they tried to have with Jimmy wouldn't end well.

What little remained of the wall was enough to show that it had been doused with accelerant. There was a glass bottle melted to the metal springs from the couch. Alcohol, sedatives, and fire equaled staged suicide. A long blade had slashed Jimmy, and the people behind the crimes were well enough acquainted with Japanese culture they knew about the white rose. Maybe, just maybe...

As he kicked at yet another pile of rubble, he finally found it. An officer's sword, probably belonging to

Masao, was buried underneath it. "So that was the big plan—make it look like he was depressed without his family, so he sat down, drank to deal with the pain, set fire to their memory, and committed harakiri. Sneaky."

"Did you say something?" Lauren called to him.

"Just thinkin' out loud is all," Kent called back.

One thing didn't fit. This was obviously arson. Everything else in the place was there to frame Masao Nagasaki for his own murder. The place hadn't spontaneously erupted in flames. If they wanted to make it look like Masao had died 'honorably', why take the containers away? And why had the man come back after disposing of them? Shouldn't that have been the last thing he did?

He kept poking at the piles of debris until he got his answer. Four empty metal gas cans, deformed from the heat, had been placed by the couch, only to be buried by a section of the ceiling.

That was all he could do for now. The soles of his shoes were smoking, and he needed to get outside to cool off.

He slipped off his loafers as soon as he got outside, enjoying the sweet relief of the icy dew. The last hour had been exhausting, and he had to take a break.

Moments after he sat on the small garden bench in

the remains of the little garden, he saw a car stop. A slight figure stood on the running board before stepping out. She looked familiar, but he couldn't remember why. Who was she?

As she stood at the house, her gloved hand daintily covering her mouth, Kent saw her tear-stained face clearly, and he suddenly remembered her. He had met her when he brought Masao Nagasaki home. "Mrs. Nagasaki!"

The woman jumped in terror at the sound of his voice, and he hurried to calm her. "Don't worry, ma'am, it's only me. Your husband hired me to get to the bottom of everything, remember?"

She dabbed her eyes with his offered handkerchief but looked as terrified as before. "Mr....Mr. Kent, right?"

Kent nodded, and she continued. "You must forgive me. My husband said—I thought they kill you. At least think you drop case."

"No ma'am. It takes more than a little scuffle and some fire to run me off."

It was hard to read her expression in the early morning light. Was he imagining things, or was she disappointed?

Chapter Seven
Missing!

MISA DABBED AT HER eyes with his handkerchief. "I come to talk to husband. He unreasonable, but I worried they try this. Poor man, this not good way to die. Of course, I not need you anymore. I sell and leave this awful place, if anybody pay for this heap."

"Sorry, ma'am. Mr. Nagasaki hired me, and only he can fire me."

She paled even more, a green tint covering her face as she clutched her throat. "But—I thought—"

"He's alive, although who knows for how long. But until he fires me or dies, I'm sticking with this case." There was no mistaking the panicked look on her face now.

"I have to sell! What about my children? They do this, they do much worse. This time, only him here. Next time, maybe not so lucky. Why he want to stay where we hated so much? He risk all our lives. My children. Before, we have house to sell. Now, nothing! I need talk to him."

"Ma'am, for your own safety, better let me relay the message."

"I perfectly capable of talking to husband!"

"Yes ma'am, but they might be watchin' ya, follow you to him, and kill ya both. Better let me handle it."

Enraged, she stomped her foot before finally relenting. "Make sure tell him this only beginning. They take his daughter, they say only bring her back if we leave. My little girl missing!"

Memories of the smiling little girl flooded his mind as he suddenly remembered more of the visit. "They took Suki?"

"Yes. When I see this, I thought—at least now I sell, leave, and get my daughter back. If you not able to convince him, I lose her. I not lose her, you understand? Tell him her blood on his hands if he stay."

She stomped back to her car and drove away.

"That seem suspicious to you too, Lars, or am I just paranoid?"

Lauren moved from the shelter of the giant Azalea. "Well, she <u>could</u> be a distraught mother. She lost her daughter and came here, discovered she lost her house, thought she lost her husband, and then went back to worrying about her daughter. That is quite an emotional roller coaster. And she apparently thought you were dead, so she had the added shock of seeing a ghost."

"Why would she think I was dead?"

"Mr. Nagasaki visited your house, and we told him about your grave condition. Maybe she inferred the rest."

Although trying to give the woman the benefit of the doubt, Lauren's voice was as hesitant as Kent's.

Kent debated for a moment, but didn't have time to think any longer. She'd soon be out of sight. "She knows me, Lars. You follow her. I'll find my way home. Call when you can and be careful."

Lauren was shocked, but scrambled to the truck before he could change his mind.

"Lars, there's a pistol behind the seat, if you need it," Kent called as loudly as he could, but she only waved, then she was gone.

He watched the taillights disappear, wondering if he'd done the right thing. She had good instincts, Jimmy had trained her to fight, and she had proven herself more than capable. She had even saved his life a few times. No matter how much he wanted to pretend like he was fine, his body constantly reminded him otherwise. He wasn't strong enough to be following anyone, let alone fight them. But he couldn't help feeling like he had sent her to the firing squad—these people were smart, ruthless, experienced, and desperate. Not a good combination for even a seasoned investigator, and certainly not good for someone just starting in the business. He had just sent her off with no backup, and all he could do was pray that he hadn't sent her marching off to her death.

Reluctantly, Kent turned away from the now-empty dirt road and back to his search. He wrote down everything about Mrs. Nagasaki and her car, just in case—although he hoped he wouldn't need it, that didn't mean he shouldn't be prepared. If anything happened, he wanted somebody to find Lauren, and the lost three days reminded him how important it was to write everything down.

Resigned to the fact that he couldn't do anything else to help her, he began studying the notes again. His conversation with Misa had sparked some memories, but everything about that day was still a blur, and he didn't remember anything about a fire. But he had a nagging feeling that he had visited with somebody that evening. Why did it have to be from the same time as his missing memory?

At first, he couldn't even remember if he had stopped

to see someone, or if they had visited him. It was infuriating and wasn't helping anything. What if it was the missing piece to solve the entire case? What if the identity of the mastermind was trapped in his mind, and all he had to do was remember? Had he gone to see them? No, that wasn't right. Somebody had come to his house. He couldn't recall who or why, but it felt right.

Deciding to take a break from the crime scene, he shifted his focus to the neighbors. The sun was waking up: hopefully they would be, too. Most had probably fled, but with any luck, Masao wasn't the only one who stayed to fight.

Door after door brought no response. He walked up one side of the street, then down the neighboring streets. Still no luck.

He diligently retraced his steps to Masao's house, knocking on every door to confirm he hadn't missed anyone. Maybe the owners were only in the shower and hadn't heard him knock the first time. Maybe they just couldn't make it to the door in time for whatever reason, or they thought he was a shoe salesman or Jehovah's Witness. Whatever the reason, he hoped the second knock would bring answers.

It didn't seem to work. Kent could barely stand, but he still had one last house to check. Leaning on the wall, he knocked, firmly at first, but then exhaustion got the better of him, and the last few taps were so timid he barely heard them himself. He didn't have the strength or energy to walk the last eight hundred feet to Masao's, so he collapsed onto the small step and leaned back.

"What you want?"

If he had the strength, he'd have jumped. As it was, all he could manage was to turn his head enough to look at her. "I'm investigating who's hurting your neighbors,"

"Better come inside to talk. Not many people still here, but ones that are here, you don't want to see."

She opened her door and hurried to help him inside. When she easily pulled him to his feet, Kent was amazed that such an elderly woman could move so fast and be so strong. And even though he had to rely on her to move indoors, she didn't stumble.

After she helped him to the couch, she eyed him curiously. "I saw you at Masao's."

"Yes ma'am, I was trying to find out who burned it."

"I do not mean now. You help him a few days ago."

Kent blinked in surprise. "You saw?"

"It is not safe to not see. Masao is honorable man from good family. Somebody must watch for him."

"How long have you known him?"

"Since he was three. I know him long time, very long

time. His family stayed for the war, but after many years, we all end up together, anyway."

This was better than Kent had hoped. As soon as his head stopped spinning, he planned to take full advantage of his lucky break. But all he could do now was hope she was as nice as she seemed while he blacked out.

†††††††††††††††††††††††††††

Lauren had easily followed her quarry. There were only a few cars on the road; few people were driving at five a.m. on New Year's Eve, but there were just enough to give her some cover. That changed as soon as they made it through town, but Lauren was careful to keep several car lengths between them. She saw the woman turn onto a dirt road and sped up to close the distance.

Soon she was on the same little path and slowed. She was right behind Misa; the dust from the road hadn't settled yet.

It was a short road; only ten miles, and Lauren followed it to the end. Strangely, she hadn't passed Misa, but there was no sign of anyone. There was nowhere to go. The empty road was behind her, the swamp in front of her, so how could the woman have simply disappeared?

She carefully maneuvered until she could turn

around. Somehow, she had missed something, and she wasn't going to stop until she discovered what.

Finally. It had been thirty minutes, but she found it. The road was little more than two ruts, but there was nowhere else she could have gone.

Lauren cautiously followed the trail. Out here, there was nobody around if something went wrong. She could easily wind up being fed to the alligators if she was captured, and nobody would know what happened. The worst part of that was knowing Kent would feel responsible for her death—and the fact she would have proved him right to doubt her abilities.

After a few of the longest, bumpiest miles she had ever been on, the road suddenly improved. Maybe this would reveal her target.

Two more miles. The brambles and brush suddenly opened into a small clearing with what looked like an old plantation house—grand in its time, but now sinking into the swampy ground, its grand marble pillars blackened with age. A shame, but not what she was looking for, unless...

There! Parked at the side of the house was Misa Nagasaki's car.

Lauren shifted into reverse until she could find somewhere to hide her car. With that finished, she quickly changed out of her heels and into her sneakers, then moved through the briars. Hopefully, she would find something to justify the intrusion.

"Give me my daughter."

The shrill voice easily pierced the sounds native to the area, but Lauren couldn't understand the reply. It was hard enough to distinguish that it was a man from her hiding spot without making out the words. She had to get closer.

Without warning, the door swung open. Desperately, Lauren scanned the area for somewhere to hide, but it was no use. She caught her breath as she realized there was nowhere to hide. No outbuildings, no shrubs, nothing. Her only hope was to dart to the end of the house and out of sight, then pray that whoever was coming out didn't already know she was there.

Lauren had never been so grateful to Kent as she was at that moment, running in comfortable tennis shoes instead of the miserable heels. At least they gave her a chance, however slim it might be.

She dove around the corner like she was sliding home in a baseball game. Her chest was tight, but she didn't have time to catch her breath now. Now she needed to be invisible.

Several agonizing moments passed before she was

certain she wasn't being followed. With that worry behind her, it was time to shift back to the offensive and find out who Misa was arguing with. Keeping her hand steady, Lauren inched her compact around the edge of the building. This trick had worked for her before; maybe it would work again.

Now she could see, but it didn't help. All Lauren got was a good view of Misa climbing into her car and leaving. She only had a split second to make her decision—follow Misa, or stay and find out who was in the house.

Misa had acted suspiciously, but the only reason to follow her was to find the missing girl. Whoever was inside obviously knew more about that than Misa did. However much she wanted to find out what Misa was hiding, it was more important to stay.

She held her breath and counted to twenty as the sound from the retreating car got quieter, hoping that the person would close the door so she could remain unseen. Instead, she heard footsteps.

There wasn't time to wait. The woods were several hundred feet away; so was the back of the house. If she made it to the woods, hopefully, she could see a face before escaping in Kent's truck.

Her heart pounded as she raced to the trees. Any hope

of seeing her pursuer vanished as she realized he was keeping pace with her. When she heard branches rustle behind her and then a voice cursing, her heart felt like it would explode. He was gaining on her. She wasn't going down without a fight, but she couldn't risk stopping to see his face. Her stomach was lurching, but she didn't have time for that either.

The briars snatched at her skirt, slowing her down. She paused to yank it free and finally glimpsed the man chasing her. He was short and stocky, but closing the gap quickly. The only advantage was that she seemed able to navigate the woods better. After all, she wasn't running blind. She was headed for the truck.

Without wasting another second looking behind her, Lauren jerked her skirt free from another briar. Ignoring the sound of the fabric tearing, she kept running for the truck.

There was the road up ahead. The truck wouldn't be far, and without the branches catching her face as she ran, she would move faster. Unfortunately, so would the man who was chasing her. She kept her hands out to avoid getting her face caught in the brambles, ignoring the pain of her flesh being pierced.

Her heart was thudding so loud she couldn't hear anything else; her chest was getting tighter with each step. There was still no time to stop. He was so close now that he yelped when she let go of a branch and it hit him in the face.

That bought her a moment. Not much time, but it would have to do. While he ranted and tried to catch his breath, she took a deep gulp of air and sprinted for the truck.

He was quiet again. The only noises were the crashing sounds of him pushing through the undergrowth, nearing the road. Lauren's fingers closed around the door handle as she struggled to open it. If he lunged, he'd get her. She scrambled into the truck and fumbled with the ignition as he grabbed her door and tried to force it open. She reversed as quickly as the truck could and drove him through the briars, hoping to shake him off. He broke the truck window and pawed at her coat while Lauren desperately kept her face shielded, determined not to let him identify her.

Everything she had ever learned—whether from her father, the many tutors he had hired for her, from Jimmy, or Kent—it was all in her mind, waiting for her to put it to use. Could she?

Her foot mashed the gas pedal to the floor. She had been in tough spots before, and she wasn't about to lose her nerve now. If she did, she'd prove Kent right. She would get herself killed and prove beyond the shadow of a doubt that she had no business in his world.

The truck screeched as she shifted into drive without slowing, and the gears made an awful metallic grinding sound as it lurched forward. Oh well; she could fix whatever she'd just broken later, if it didn't cause her to break down first.

It was getting hard to breathe. The man was hanging onto her coat tighter than ever, trying not to fall. She couldn't go any faster on this road, but it wouldn't be long before she hit the pavement.

No way to wait that long. She was getting lightheaded from the lack of oxygen; she had to do something now. Going faster wouldn't be possible, so she stomped the brakes.

With a shout, the man stumbled headlong into the brambles, finally releasing his grip on her as he flailed forward. Not a second to waste; he was already trying to grab her again. She ducked as his arm swiped the air where she had just been, his hot breath mingling with the cold air. One chance, and it was now or never. She mashed the accelerator to the floor, sending chunks of dirt and gravel flying at him and sending him scurrying for cover.

His angry cursing filled the silence as she sped away.

Once she was certain he had stopped chasing her, Lauren took a quick peek in her rearview mirror. She wasn't going through all of this for nothing, and now she was rewarded with her first good look at the man. His bulging eyes were red with fury, the veins on his forehead poking out, and he was angrily shaking his fist as he yelled after her. She had never seen him, but the evil glint in his eyes ensured she would never forget him.

Even as she heaved a sigh of relief, Lauren shuddered. That had been a close call, and she had little to show for it. At least she had confirmed Misa's story about the missing girl, but Lauren had lost her. Somehow, she still didn't trust the woman, even if her story was true. But there was time for that later; now it was time to find Kent, compare notes, and hope that his day had been more productive than hers.

††††††††††††††††††††††††††

KENT WOKE UP WITH a start as he tried to remember where he was. Wiping the sleep out of his eyes, he looked around for something—anything—to jog his memory. Nothing looked familiar. The room was bare, but warm; a soft brown color had a calming effect, but did nothing to help him figure out where he was.

A slight coughing sound brought his focus to a

chair opposite him; the woman staring at him looked familiar. He was getting so tired of thinking that! He was a detective, and it was his job to remember things. Lately, it seemed like he was lucky to remember his name.

She waited politely for him to gather himself, and he finally recognized her. The memories came flooding back, and he was ready to cash in on his lucky break now. *At least she didn't kill me while I was out.* Out loud he said, "Thanks for the couch, ma'am. Sorry about...well, everything."

She nodded. "Why are you here?"

"Work."

"Well, she did not bring you here, and you helped him."

"Okay, I'll bite. Why her and not him?"

"She very determined to get home, and he wants only to stay away from there. Very bad memories for him. She want her family to only speak Japanese, think Japanese, but he wants balance. Honor where he from, but respect where he is. He says the children must know the horror of the past so they do not grow up, make the same mistake. He also very careful. Tell them to be as much like you as possible to keep this from happening."

"You don't think much of her, huh?" Kent had finally

managed to sit up and had used his hands to prop up his head. He didn't feel strong enough to sit with nothing supporting him yet, and he wasn't sure he wouldn't fall back any moment.

The woman didn't answer, continuing to stare past him, lost in her own thoughts.

"What's been happening to your neighbors?"

"We are being exterminated. We have done nothing to deserve this, but have suddenly become the yokai you fear."

"Any idea what changed?" Kent's head had finally stopped whirling enough he could jot down a few notes in his book again.

The woman shrugged. "Perhaps any number of things. We were never honored guests here, but I have never seen what happens now, at least not since the camps. I now have seen three families buried and six more run away in fear."

"Ever see who did it?"

"Always I see. It is a group, between four and eight, wearing all white. They do different things depending on how many times they have already come. But surely Masao tell you all this already? Few stay as long as Masao, but he protect those of us left. Without him, we have nothing."

She spoke in a matter-of-fact tone that Kent was all too familiar with—the hopeless resignation that fate had already decided to be done with you. He'd been feeling that way himself lately, but somehow, he was still alive.

Having come this far, he felt obligated to help her as well. "Ma'am, I can't tell you who's been doin' this yet, but I aim to find out. The Nagasakis are out of danger, and now, we need to get you somewhere safe, too. I'll stay and watch your house. That'll let me see who they are."

"No. I do not think that you can help us, and I do not know you. For all I know, you made him disappear, and will do same to me."

"I promise, ma'am..."

"I not think you did, but the point remains. To be honest, I do not believe you strong enough, even if you want only to help. Please accept my most humble apologies, but I speak only the truth."

Kent swallowed hard. "I ain't been told I wasn't man enough to do something in a long time."

"I apologize, that not what I mean."

"Yeah, I know, but it is what you said. And what's worse, you're partly right. But I aim to prove you wrong. I'll take you to Nagasaki, and after you two talk, you can decide if you trust me."

"It is very unlikely you change my mind, but I will go with you."

The woman led the way to her car, and they left. Although he was wary of being seen when he drove to the hospital, he was twice as careful as he entered Masao's room. For anybody to associate him with the enemy was unthinkable, but he had a job to do, and a client who needed him.

He had three motives for visiting the man. One was to gain her trust—if he could stay in the house of the sole holdout, he would have front-row seats to the final attack. The second was to see if Masao trusted her. The third was the most important to him, no matter how he tried to ignore it. Masao needed a friendly face; nobody should be alone after going through so much.

Once satisfied he had accomplished everything, he left the two reminiscing about old times and hurried to Jimmy's room for a quick visit.

Jimmy was still groggy, but Kent wasn't planning on a long stay, anyway. He had to get back to Mrs. Watanabe's house; if Lauren returned home and he wasn't there, she would be worried. He needed to talk to her, but he couldn't waste any more time. If he did, he might miss his chance to catch the attackers.

Hours passed. The sun set with no sign of the young woman, and his calls to her house went unanswered. He was getting worried; he still hadn't heard from her. Every doubt he ever had was screaming 'I told you so' in his head, worrying him more with each passing moment. It was New Year's Eve; he was supposed to be spending it with her, not pacing by the window.

What a fool he had been! He knew he hadn't imagined that conversation with her. It had replayed in his head, over and over, each time becoming a little bit clearer. And she had all but confirmed it after agreeing to take care of him. He had risked that for what? To help somebody too stubborn to leave when they weren't wanted? Fine, that was an oversimplification. The case was a worthy one, no matter who the client was, but he shouldn't have sent her to work on it. Maybe she'd be ready in a few years, but not yet. Now, instead of them celebrating the new year together, he had sent her off to get killed.

Finally, at eight o'clock, he saw headlights and peeked through the curtains. At first, nothing. Not surprising, since Lauren would be wary of an ambush and had no idea where he was. And if it was someone planning to hurt the elderly owner of the house, they would certainly stay in the shadows.

A figure darted through the darkness, moving from bush to dying bush until it reached the shelter of the Nagasaki house, now reduced to ash and charred wood. It was too dark to tell any more about who it could be from the darkness of his post, so he moved around to the back of the house.

It didn't take long to close the distance between the door and the ruins. A surprised yelp sounded as he jerked the figure into the moonlight, and then he doubled in pain when a blow landed at the base of his ribs.

"Wait, William?"

Kent held his hand up as he caught his breath. He wheezed, but finally managed to talk. "That answers that. Glad you're back, kid. Next time, have a heart—I'm already beat."

"I didn't know that it was you. Why are you still here?"

"Probably the same reason you are, except I've got a nice warm house to do it from. I was beginnin' to think you were gonna stand me up."

"Ha! You wish you could get rid of me that easily. You ought to know that if you have not run me off already, when I had a steady, you never will. Why would I wait to stand you up until I was stuck with you?"

He pulled her close, and they walked arm-in-arm into the house, the detective keeping watch on the shadows and carefully avoiding springing his own traps.

Once inside, the two began comparing notes. It was certainly not the most glamorous part of the job, but it was necessary. Now was the time to see who had found what, and by the time they finished, the chatter on the radio had silenced and the moon was high in the sky.

A quick glance at his watch—eleven fifty-five. "Sorry, Lars, not the start to the new year I had in mind."

Lauren slipped her dainty hand into his large one. "You must have loftier plans than what you shared with me. You promised we would spend it together, and here we are. Given your tendency to get into trouble, the fact that you are even awake exceeds my expectations, and is most certainly all I could hope for."

She snuggled next to him as the fireworks started, and watched in astonishment as the unflappable detective began sweating and trembling. Not knowing what else to do, she gripped his hand and put her arm around his waist.

The celebration finally ended, and several minutes later, his rapid breathing finally slowed. His shoulders sagged in defeat as he smiled apologetically. "Sorry, Lars, I probably should've just gone to bed. Reckon I'll leave you be. G'night."

Lauren gently snagged his arm as he moved away, pulling him back toward her. "Just where do you think you are going?"

"Well, I—well, I've been enough trouble for one night."

He looked so much like a scared little boy that her heart broke for him. Gently she brushed a shock of his curly hair back into its proper place, then cupped his face in her hands. "William Kent, this is where I chose to be. I. Chose. You. Do you hear me? You, with your beautiful mess. You are always there for me, remember? Even though you shouldn't have been. You should've run. But you stuck by me and saved me. So you don't like fireworks. Big deal. We'll just spend loud holidays somewhere quiet. See? Problem solved. That's what I do—solve your problems."

She grabbed his hat and put it on her head, setting it askance before putting her hand on her hip and wagging her finger at him. "And you best come up with a better way to get rid of me. You are not going to scare me off—I'm enjoying our job too much."

Kent arched his eyebrows, earning a laugh from Lauren before she spoke again. "You got me. Now, you go get some rest, and I will take the first watch."

When he hesitated, she propelled him toward the makeshift bed he had made for himself.

The night passed quietly, and morning came. Lauren wasn't sure whether Kent was relieved or disappointed that it had been so uneventful. Honestly, she wasn't even sure how she felt. An intruder could give them a lead, and she wasted a perfectly good night's sleep for nothing. But surely they could find a lead without risking life and limb. Couldn't they?

After a brief discussion, they had their battle plan. Divide and conquer—Jimmy was awake and would go home in a few hours. Lauren's job was to interview him and fill in any missing details she could. Kent was going to track down the oh-so-glorious paper trail to find out who owned the properties now. They were to be finished and meet back at their new headquarters at six p.m., no matter what. Kent grinned as he remembered Lauren's parting words: "No excuse for missing the deadline is acceptable. You can show up early with roses, but you had better not let anything make you late, or I will make you suffer."

Kent had smirked. "Even if I'm dead?"

"Especially then."

She had seen him at his most vulnerable and was still sticking with him. If she thought he was worth a second chance, maybe he was. She was one of the smartest people he knew, after all. He gave everybody else another shot at redemption—even his former enemy. Why didn't he do the same for himself? Was he really worse than an Imperial soldier?

He pored over the deeds for each property. Although he was certain that the recent attacks stemmed from something completely unrelated to the history of the land, Kent still wanted to be thorough.

Welp, wasted time on that. Kent set aside the mountain of papers he had been studying and moved to the archives. Even though he had low expectations, he scrutinized every microfilm with great care.

Disappointing though it was, he wasn't surprised to discover that he had wasted his time on that, too. He verified the claim Masao's neighbor had made about the deaths, although there was little information in the obituaries. Most of them contained only the usual platitudes, indifferent to anything personal, refusing to give even the slightest hint of sympathy; the articles glazed over the murders as 'natural causes'. He involuntarily clutched his ribs; there was nothing natural about any of it.

Finally. It had been a boring day; he was lucky the clerk was sweet on him or he wouldn't have been able to get as much information as he had. For a moment he wondered how his date had changed things—should he feel guilty for leading the girl on? No, he had offered nothing other than a smile and hello. But better find out exactly what his relationship was. It had been seventeen years, and he was only just feeling ready to start seeing a special someone again. And he hoped that someone was Lauren.

Enough mush; get a grip, fella. One absolutely awful date and you're gaga. It doesn't matter if she turns you down. She's only one fish. You can find another, now that you're looking.

Although he was back at Mrs. Watanabe's house thirty minutes early, he opened the door to an aroma that made his mouth water. The tantalizing scent led him to the kitchen, where he quickly discovered its origin.

Lauren was pulling a steaming hot tuna casserole out of the oven, a basket of fresh rolls on the table next to the orange-honey glazed carrots, baked sweet potatoes, green beans with fatback, and sauteed squash. With two candles lit, she clearly had bigger plans for this meal than just filling her stomach.

"Excellent timing; I'm pleased you chose to be punctual for once."

They silently enjoyed the meal, while Kent replayed the events of the last three days. This wasn't the time for romance, it was the time for finding whoever was hunting families before they hunted <u>his</u> family.

"Earth to William. Are you with me?"

He jumped before looking across the table. Lauren had cleared the table and now had Waldorf salad, banana pudding, and congealed salad on the table with fresh dessert plates. *What did I miss?*

"I asked if it wasn't time to make me an official part of your detective agency, since my duties have expanded from secretary. Perhaps even make me a partner. I think I have proven myself well enough to get at least the title."

Kent nearly choked on his water, quickly moving the napkin to clean his face.

"Honestly. I know you are against me working with you, but such vulgarity."

Kent exhaled. "Shouldn't you put in a few more years? Jimmy ain't even a partner, long as we've known each other."

"Yes, but I spend half my time playing nursemaid to you and the other half cleaning up your messes. That makes you my full-time job, which should be enough to earn the title."

The two finally reached a compromise. Lauren would become a detective temporarily, and they would see how she liked her new role. Kent congratulated himself on keeping silent and not making a fool of himself—how had he made such a mistake? How had he imagined, for even a second, that there was anything more between them than a working companionship?

Even if he had completely misread the entire evening, he needed to know exactly how to define their relationship. Now, more than ever, he wanted to know the answer. "So, Lars, before we—I mean, well, are we—what I mean is,"

Lauren kept a straight face while watching him blunder through the conversation. She was enjoying his fumbling immensely and having too much fun to help him find the right words.

After several awkward moments, Kent decided the direct approach would be the best. "Are we goin' steady?"

"Well, William, I can only handle one job at a time, especially one as demanding as this."

His face flushed red. "That's not what I mean."

"Oh! Well, I suppose the answer is the same. There's only so much a girl can handle, right?"

"That's one way of putting it." Kent pretended

to pout, but she had said enough. He had verbal confirmation; she was only seeing him.

From there, the conversation turned back to the case. With the updated information, they spread out the notes and began a timeline.

Copies of the obituaries were placed in their spots, and soon they had everything—everything except the answers. Why? Who? Why now? It didn't make sense, and the only thing that connected the new owners was that they bought the properties cheap as soon as the old owners left. It was suspicious, but not enough.

When Kent glanced up at Lauren, she was stifling a yawn. He promptly sent her to bed before settling into his post for the night, hopeful for a glimpse of the people behind the threats.

One o'clock, two o'clock, three o'clock. Nothing. Four o'clock. Still nothing. Then, at four-thirty, he saw somebody sneaking up to the Nagasaki house.

Quietly, he slipped outside and toward the ruins. The figure was slight and unsteady. This didn't seem like some enemy returning to see their handiwork. He had a hunch, and following it would either save him a lot of trouble or get him killed. His life was just getting interesting. He couldn't risk it being the latter, and could only hope that it was the former.

Chapter Eight
Arrested

"M R. NAGASAKI?"

The figure stopped short before stepping into the dim moonlight. "Detective-san?"

"Come on, ain't nothing for you here. Is your neighbor with you?"

"Yes, she is in the car. I told her to wait for me until I return."

"Well then, let's get y'all inside, double-time."

The threesome was soon safely inside her home, sitting at the table while studying the timeline the detectives had prepared. A few adjustments were made, and finally, the first attack was confirmed.

From there, Kent confirmed the pattern. If he was right and the death of the young thugs hadn't changed the timetable, the next day would bring the killers to him; it was time for the cross to be burned in her yard.

Of course, they could just decide to be finished with the façade. There was only one person between them and ownership of the entire neighborhood. If they decided to just kill her and be done with it, they could come to kill him at any minute. Well, let them come. If they hurried, Kent could identify them and end everything.

"Detective-san, do you hear me?"

Kent jumped, startled by the interruption. "Sorry, pal. Run that by me one more time."

"Hai. I ask if you know where my family is."

"That won't make a difference."

"It will to me. Where is my family?"

"Your wife took your kids."

"Are they safe?"

Kent hesitated. The man had gone through so much, and he couldn't do anything to help find Suki. "Yes, mostly."

The relieved expression that had been creeping onto Masao's face vanished, replaced by one of fear. "Mostly?"

Again Kent paused. The revelation would bring only pain to his former enemy, but it was his family. He deserved to know. And as much as Kent hated it, there was a part of him—a bigger part than he wanted to admit—that enjoyed Masao's suffering. The camps still felt like yesterday, along with all the inhumanity he had suffered because of people like the man standing in front of him. Yet that man, who still believed his cause to be just, was now in <u>his</u> country, living what had been a good life until 'this', whatever 'this' was. He felt a surge of heat as his face flushed hot with anger; maybe this man deserved what he was getting.

No. Masao Nagasaki might have deserved to suffer for his part in the war, but he wasn't one of those guards. He hadn't been responsible for any of it. He was a soldier who had served his country. In that respect, they were the same. And even if Masao Nagasaki deserved this, he wasn't the one paying for whatever sins he might have committed; a little girl full of sunshine was suffering, too. If the roles were reversed, he'd hope that somebody wouldn't hold his past against Rita O'Sullivan, or torture her because her father was Irish. What kind of man would he be if he left Suki to die because of her father?

"Look, I'm all over it, but somebody took Suki."

All the defeat that had stooped Masao's shoulders was gone, and every muscle was now tense with determination. "Someone took my daughter, and you did not tell me? Did you plan on ever telling me this?"

Kent leaned back, arms crossed, and locked eyes with Masao. "Never."

Masao blinked at the matter-of-fact response. "You have no right. How dare you keep my family from me?"

"Look, can you tell me anything new about what's happened?"

"I already tell you everything."

"Do you know who took her?"

"The people who are targeting me."

"And they are?"

Masao remained rigid. "How do I know? I tell you everything already."

"Exactly. Did me tellin' you change anythin'? Are we any closer to findin' Suki?"

"No." Masao's shoulders sagged once more, his hands shaking as he was forced to admit the truth. "But it is my right to know. It is my family."

After a few hours of back and forth, Masao and Mrs. Watanabe left for a hotel, leaving Kent and the soundly asleep Lauren alone in the house again. The lights were turned out according to the everyday schedule of Mrs. Chiyoki Watanabe to avoid arousing the suspicions of anyone watching.

The morning arrived with little fanfare after another tedious stakeout. As the sun's golden rays peeked through the windows, Kent rubbed his eyes, frustrated about the wasted night. So much else he could have done. He moved back to his makeshift desk, hoping to find something he had missed. Maybe he could still salvage the night.

Forty minutes later, Lauren came out, freshly showered and hair perfectly coiffed, as usual. "Well, somebody had a productive night."

"Not really, but I got one thing done, anyway. Got the timeline nailed down, so that's something, at least."

Intrigued, Lauren almost sat next to him. Instead, she started breakfast, and Kent explained what he had learned. then insisted Kent eat; as soon as he took his last bite she sent him to bed. "I'll keep working. You don't have to worry about that. A fresh set of eyes will help, and after you sleep, you can get back to work. You are still recovering, you know."

Although Kent protested vehemently, he eventually gave up and followed orders, leaving Lauren to watch for anything out of the ordinary. With nothing else to do, she made call after call, hoping to find something that Kent hadn't. Hopefully, she could find out what the owners had in common, or at least find Mrs. Nagasaki. She wanted to talk to the suspicious woman herself, woman to woman, and learn what she was hiding. Maybe if Lauren could confront her without Kent there, she could find the truth. Maybe.

I am not looking forward to this bill. Lauren grimaced at the thought; there were so many long-distance calls. It made more sense than visiting each hotel in person, and all the walking that would eventually entail. Kent might work that way, but that didn't mean she had to. Besides, wasn't he the one who said 'Work smarter, not harder'?

She tried every hotel, motel, and inn within three hundred miles. And finally, in Sarasota, she got lucky. A family had checked in two days before that exactly fit the description of the missing Nagasaki clan. She began thinking as she hung up the phone. The killers shouldn't show up at the house until around eleven; she could call to wake Kent around nine, and he would have plenty of time to prepare. A quick note telling Kent her plans and she was off—she couldn't wait for the interstate President Eisenhower wanted. It should shorten the drive considerably.

For now, she would have to be content with the long route. At least it was a change from her usual scenery. St. Augustine was beautiful, there was no denying that, but she had spent most of her life moving from one country to another. This was the longest she had ever been in one spot; aside from the trip to Virginia she had taken with Doris and Liza Jane, she hadn't left the state in two years.

By one p.m., she was at the hotel. The clerk who had been so friendly on the phone was much less gullible in person and refused to tell her anything more about the family.

What next? Lauren was so close; there was no way she was giving up now and going home empty-handed. Knocking on every door in the hotel would likely only get her a police escort home; she wouldn't get any answers that way, either.

So now it was time to settle in for the inevitable stakeout. Her life had certainly changed in the past two years! One minute was complete boredom, while the next could bring panic-inducing terror. There was an undeniable thrill to solving the puzzle, and an even bigger thrill if she could solve it before Kent.

That was exactly what she planned to do. Even if she had to sit in a car with a forty-degree chill all night.

At least she had a blanket and her Hit Parader magazine—Debbie Reynolds made the best movies; the Chordettes and Doris Day were in this issue, too. That should take the chill off her surroundings. Pulling the scarf tighter around her ears, she began her vigil as nonchalantly as possible.

Like Kent, she was in for a long wait. As the afternoon

slowly melted into the night, the chill in the air made her regret not bringing any food, or at least a warm thermos. Mmm...she could be sipping on some nice, hot cocoa right now, warming her frozen fingers with the container. Just thinking about it made her mouth water, and she could almost smell the chocolate.

Well, she hadn't planned that far ahead, and there was nothing she could do about it now except to make a mental note for next time and ignore the rumbling in her stomach.

Night eased by slowly. Nothing. She had called Kent with the disappointing news twice and was scheduled to check in again in another forty minutes; they were both having an unproductive night. For whatever reason, nobody was at her house yet.

It was after midnight; too dark to read, and too cold to keep the windows closed—she'd had to open them after they started fogging up. She shivered and turned her coat collar up, never taking her eyes off of the door.

Movement! Somebody was creeping out the back door. Lauren slid as far down in the back seat as she could while still watching. Maybe she wasn't on a fool's errand after all. She couldn't make the person out; was it Misa Nagasaki, or somebody random?

Finally. Her patience was rewarded when the slight

figure paused at Misa Nagasaki's car and looked toward her. It almost felt like the woman was looking straight at Lauren, but that was impossible. Lauren had parked the truck discreetly, and it was too dark for the woman to see inside the cab. The sleuth shuddered involuntarily at the thought of being caught, but remained crouched low.

Mrs. Nagasaki pulled away, and the chase was on—a very slow chase. The drive was mind-numbingly boring, punctuated by moments of adrenaline when she disappeared around a curve or turned into a well-hidden road. Thirty minutes later, she stopped.

They were in the middle of nowhere; there was not even a house in the lonely swamp, but she had chosen that location to stop. When Mrs. Nagasaki moved into the darkness, Lauren cautiously followed. Why were they here?

In the darkness, it was hard to keep her suspect in sight. The woman's choice of clothing made it even harder; she was wearing a dark wool coat and hat. Yet Lauren stayed right behind her, never far enough away for the footsteps to disappear into the noises of the swamp.

Sudden silence. Why had the rustling stopped? The woman was out of sight, forcing Lauren to make a decision. She took a deep, silent breath and stepped forward into an explosion of light, then crumpled to the ground.

†††††††††††††††††††††††††††

THERE WAS A THROBBING pain in Lauren's head as she slowly woke up. But it wasn't just the pounding in her skull that was bothering her. There was something else. A burning ache surged through her body in waves; one moment so intense it was blinding and all-consuming, and the next moment it ebbed slightly. She was moving; she could feel the rough terrain tearing at her skin before turning into squishy mud, then from dirt to grass. As she focused, she realized somebody was dragging her by her hair. That explained the strange ache in her head, at least, but who was doing this to her?

She started trying to wriggle free. No good; her hands were tied behind her back. Moving her legs confirmed they were bound too. What to try next?

Suddenly, she couldn't breathe. Her throat had something around it, pulling tighter and making her eyes burn as she desperately gasped for air. No time for second-guessing now; she would either free herself or die. Her body was quickly being lifted off the ground and her head getting giddy. She was desperately straining to reach her pocket, and finally managed to close her fingers around the pen she always carried there. It had been a gag gift from Kent after Mac's poison pen letters had almost gotten them all killed, but she planned to put it to use now.

A final twist and it was open. The tip fell away to reveal a sharp knife; as her feet left the ground, she swung her body back with all her strength, thrusting the knife as she felt his flesh brush against hers. The ropes bit into her flesh, causing Lauren to gasp in pain.

Her attacker relaxed his grasp on the rope, and she fell to the ground with a thud. She couldn't waste time catching her breath; he could regain his hold at any moment, and then all would be lost. Leaning against a tree for support, Lauren sawed the little knife through the ropes still holding her prisoner. Her attacker was making an odd wheezing sound; she wasn't worried about being recaptured now. Now she was worried about taking the man alive.

By the time her hands were free and she could see clearly enough to find her would-be killer, he was dead. Somehow, her wild backward thrust while flailing in the air had landed in his neck.

A few minutes more and none of the ropes remained. She quickly removed the rope from her neck and wound it around her shoulder, avoiding any glimpse of the body on the ground, then stumbled off to find her truck.

Even though she was still wheezing, Lauren was worried about another ambush. Finally. The Nagasaki car was in sight, her truck would be nearby. Since the windows were fogged up, it was a safe bet she had just found Misa Nagasaki.

Being careful to stay hidden, she paused. Panting would only alert her quarry to her presence, so she caught her breath before creeping up to the Nagasaki car, armed with the pistol she had taken from the dead man. Adrenaline pulsed through her body, erasing the exhaustion that had overwhelmed her moments before as she braced for an ambush of her own.

Using her best Hepburn impersonation, she prepared to confront the woman.

"All right, sister, reach for the sky!"

"Oh! You startle me."

"I'll do more than that if you don't do what I say. Get out now, lady, or regret it!"

"But I—I only come to find my daughter. That all. I did not know you were there..."

"Go sell your story to somebody else. That guy knew I was coming."

Misa's lip trembled, but she raised her chin defiantly. "Maybe he wait for me, only get you first."

"How big a fool do you think I am? I followed you here, see, so he couldn't have got me by mistake."

Lauren opened the trunk and motioned for the woman to sit. Quickly, she tied Misa up, shoved her inside, fastened the trunk, and headed home.

†††††††††††††††††††††††††††

Kent was pacing by the window. Lauren's last phone call had been before midnight, and she had insisted he needed rest. They finally compromised: if nobody had showed up by two o'clock, he would go to her house and they would meet at 2:30. She had missed her last check-in; now she missed their meeting by nearly five hours. Where was she?

Seeing headlights shine through the window, Kent knocked a lamp off the table in his mad rush to pull the curtains. If it wasn't Lauren, it was bad news.

Kent sighed in relief. It wasn't her car, but she had flashed the headlights using their pre-arranged signal. And now that he knew she was safe, he was ready to give her a piece of his mind.

He cleared the steps in one bound and the long drive in three, fully intending to lecture her on the dangers of being alone. When he opened the door and saw her, his anger gave way to fear again; even though she had carefully concealed the marks on her neck, she was disheveled and unfocused.

Kent held up three fingers, demanding an answer. "How many?"

She huffed and brushed his hand aside. "Please, William, I am not daft."

When she refused to answer, he scooped her up and stumbled inside. Her slight weight was almost too much for him, but he was determined to help her. After all, she always helped him.

After several minutes, he finally made it to her bed, dropping her in unceremoniously before plopping down by her feet to catch his breath. He didn't allow much time for that; she still needed him. He scurried to make her comfortable, propping her up before questioning her.

She shook her head. "William, I learned little, and am too tired to tell you most of it, but when I followed Mrs. Nagasaki, she led me into a trap. She insisted that she is innocent, and that I had walked into something meant for her, but I do not believe her. Do with that knowledge what you will after you take her out of the trunk of her car. Now, I am following your advice and going to sleep."

Kent wasn't used to being on this side of the hospital bed. He had led a rough life, which had often landed him flat on his back, but it wasn't often that something happened to Mac or Jimmy. On the rare occasion one of his friends needed help, Doris was always there.

Not this time. This time it was all on him. He put her in danger by getting her involved in the first place; it didn't matter that she had stumbled onto the case and refused to back down, or that he was too weak to work it without her.

Actually, the last part mattered a lot. She would never have learned about his case if he had been stronger or smarter. Then he had let her go off on her own to work his job because he was still too feeble to do it himself. She had good instincts, but was still new to his world—until five years ago, the toughest decision she had to make was what college to attend. Now he had dumped her in deep waters filled with sharks, and she might as well be wearing a bathing suit made of chum; his conscience was working overtime for that miscalculation.

Well, learn and move on. He could kick himself later. Now he needed to pick up where she had left off. He got Misa Nagasaki out of the trunk, carried her inside, dumped her on the couch, and called Masao.

As soon as Masao entered the room, the woman's face paled. "B-b-but, you-you said..."

Kent shrugged and glanced at his client. "I may have let her think you were worse off than you were." Turning back to Misa, he studied her intently. "Now, ma'am, I'm goin' to ask ya somethin'. Were you in my house a few days ago?"

Misa jumped, her eyes darting furtively around the room as she looked for a way out. With no escape and unsure of what Kent knew, she decided to remain silent.

Lauren beckoned Kent over to her eavesdropping post from the hallway to hand him her glove and the little bag she had placed it in. "When we were at your home, the morning after you were attacked, I felt my glove slide over something gooey. I cleaned it to ensure that Mrs. Williams and Mr. Campbell wouldn't be inconvenienced any further, and I meant to have Lieutenant Sloane test it. But my constant worrying about you caused me to lose focus and eventually made me physically ill. Finally, I found this comb in your chair. Show them to her and bluff; see what she knows."

Kent accepted her evidence before shooing her back to bed and returning to the task at hand.

"I found this Kushi comb in my house, so I know you were there. I don't know anybody else who has one."

Misa quickly looked away, but her husband confirmed it was hers. She knew then that lying was pointless, and answered in a barely audible whisper, "Yes."

"Mrs. Nagasaki, I was poisoned the night you visited me. Do you know anything about that?"

"No!"

"I found some gunk on my doorknob, and that's how the poison was administered. I don't suppose you know anything about that, either?"

Again, she denied it.

"The comb has the same gunk that my doorknob did. My guess is, you had it on your gloves so you wouldn't poison yourself, but transferred it to your comb when you were fidgeting with it on your way out the door. What do you have to say about that?"

Her eyes flashed dangerously. "That's a lie! I never touch it at door. It maybe fall out when I talk to you, but not after I—"

Realizing what she had done, Misa abruptly stopped talking, but it was too late. Kent had trapped her, and she knew it.

"I only do it to save Suki. They tell me, I kill you, or they kill her. My daughter or a round eye? No contest."

Masao's jaw dropped. "Onna!"

She studiously ignored him and repeated herself. "Choice between life of my daughter or man who killed my friends was not choice."

"They didn't have her then,"

"They able to get her alone to threaten her. That enough proof for me. When I fail, they go after husband. I try to keep my family safe, but it no good. They find us and take her, say sell or they kill her."

Kent was still suspicious. "How did you know about him?"

"They say they kill him."

"How many people threatened you?"

"I only ever see one."

Lauren called Kent back to the hallway, and he was beginning to get frustrated. "Now see here, Lars. I told you to stay in bed."

"This cannot wait, William. I saw her talking to someone at that house, and it was definitely not the same person who I—the one I saw at the—well, it was not the man who attacked me."

"Thanks."

Kent scooped her up and carried her back to bed, once again sweating profusely and wheezing by the time he had her safely nestled under her covers. She was blissfully unaware of his struggles; before he had even set her down, she was sound asleep. That gave him a minute to rest before returning to the Nagasakis.

After he caught his breath, he walked down the hall, but paused to study the couple from Lauren's hiding spot. Masao appeared to be genuinely horrified by his wife's matter-of-fact attitude toward the attempted murder, and the two had positioned themselves as far apart as the couch allowed.

A sudden wave of dizziness washed over Kent again, and he leaned against the wall for support. *I've gotta remember not to get poisoned again. This is for the birds! Carry a tiny little thing like Lars to her room, and now I'm pantin' like a fish outta water. This ain't for sissies, I know that. Hopefully, from now on, anybody that tries to kill me does it the normal way and tries to stab me, shoot me, or just bashes me over the head. I hate bein' weak!*

Once he could control his breathing again, Kent decided he had learned everything he could from observing the couple. Moving back into the room, he resumed his interrogation.

"So, Mrs. Nagasaki, you mixed up the poison yourself?"

"No, they give it to me."

"I thought you only saw one?"

Misa squirmed. "I did!"

"My colleague saw two in as many days. You met with one, and the other attacked her."

"Who you mean? Crazy woman who lock me in trunk? She say I see two?"

"She said there was a second person in the woods."

"I supposed to meet somebody, but he not there. Finally, I go wait in car, then crazy lady show up with gun."

"And you didn't see or hear anything?"

The woman sniffed disdainfully. "I already tell you that. Why you not listen?"

"Well, if that's all you got to say, I'll be turnin' you in now."

"For what?" Misa stammered.

"Let's start with tryin' to off me. How about that? Maybe they can keep you outta trouble at the police station."

Her eyes opened wide in terror as she clutched her throat. "B-but, I only do it for my daughter. Tell him, husband. It only for my Suki."

Masao turned his head from her, his face devoid of emotion. "There is no honor in what you have done. You have brought shame upon my house, and for what? They have still taken my little girl, regardless of your treachery. Had you not attempted to kill the only man helping us, they would not have taken her, and my little Suki would be safe in her own bed now, or at least safely concealed from them."

"You so high and mighty!" Misa screeched. "You leave us to mercy of wicked men to protect your house. All I do is protect my family, and this how you treat me?"

Coldly, Masao locked eyes with her. "Whom did you protect?"

At first, Misa had no reply, and could only hang her head in shame. That soon changed, and she defiantly mumbled, "Still more than you do."

Kent called Sloane, then roughly pulled her to her feet and began dragging her toward the front door, his hand clasped tightly around her wrist. He was tired of this game and ready for answers. If she wouldn't give them to him, she could give them to Sloane.

She wasn't yet ready to give up. Misa dug her heels into the thick carpet, pushing against him with all her strength. "What about my daughter? I who they talk to. I only one who ever see them. What you do without me?"

"Mrs. Nagasaki, as 'helpful' as you have been, I am certain we can muddle through without you."

Misa deflated completely, then collapsed in a faint.

Although his first instinct was to let her fall, Kent caught her and moved her back to the couch, then moved to get her a glass of water.

There was a knock on the front door, and Kent turned to his client. "Watch her while I go see who that is, and be sure to watch your back."

Masao nodded, and Kent hurried to the door. "Sloane? What brings you here?"

"Technically, I'm not here. I could get into a world of trouble for this."

"That sounds serious."

"It is. Remember your nosy neighbor?"

"Boy howdy, do I. She has nothing better to do with her life than to make mine hell."

"Might not wanna say that next time somebody asks about her. They did a welfare check and found her dead. Somebody put their hand over her mouth and held it there until she shut up for good."

Kent's jaw dropped.

"That's a good expression. Use that when they question you. You're suspect numero uno."

"But-me? Why me? I'da killed the battle ax years ago if she bothered me that much."

"Don't use that as your defense, whatever you do. She was gettin' ready to testify against you. I'm certain it was bogus, and Irish pieced together a lot of answers for you, but she claims you attacked those kids, and not the other way around. And even though I can't prove it,

I know Irish found those bodies before we did. If they find out, they'll say you sent him to sanitize the scene, then offed her to cover it up."

"Wait, sanitize what? What are you talking about? What kids?"

"The ones that jumped you a few nights back."

Kent stared at his friend, completely bewildered.

"Wow. Irish said you couldn't remember, but wow. How do you kill eight guys and not remember it?"

The news was too much for Kent, who collapsed backward onto the wall.

Sloane rushed to steady his friend, studying him intently. "Irish didn't tell you, did he?"

Kent shook his head while trying to remember anything. Why hadn't Jimmy told him? If the police had found the delinquents, he was confident his friend had. So why keep it hidden? Was the old woman right? If he had been as near death as his friends said, it seemed impossible that he could have fought off eight people. None of it made any sense.

A crackling noise was coming from Sloane's radio, so he steered the unsteady detective toward the car. They arrived just in time to hear a patrol unit dispatched to pick Kent up, which was the last thing the policeman wanted; they'd find him there, and he'd immediately be thrown off the case. He quickly radioed back that he'd do it, hoping to keep Kent safe from any rash officers who might respond.

Turning to his friend, he gripped Kent's shoulder reassuringly. "Look, they're fishing right now. Don't give 'em anything, and for pity's sake, act surprised. Honest, I know you didn't do it. I owe you and Irish my life, so let me help you. Let me take you in so somebody doesn't get trigger-happy."

"We both know the investigation starts and ends with me."

"If only you knew somebody who could help with that. A gumshoe, maybe—oh, wait. You literally have one on the payroll."

"Two. Lauren's convinced me to add her. But I can't get locked up, Sloane. I just can't."

"Easy. Nobody said anything about locking you up. I'll make sure you stay at my desk when you're not being questioned. Just 'cause they think I'm weak now doesn't mean I can't still pull rank, and I can throw my weight around with the best of them if need be. I've trusted you plenty, Kent. Now you gotta trust me."

"But how am I gonna tell Jimmy anything? He can't help if I don't get him word, and you know he got stabbed. And Lars took a nasty hit. Mrs. Williams isn't here, but my client is. I can't just leave her here by herself."

"I'll send Irish over as soon as we pass a phone booth, but if you don't go in with me, it's only gonna get worse for you."

Kent's shoulders sagged dejectedly as he squeezed into the back seat of Sloane's '57 Police Pursuit, feeling as though he were being marched back to Sandakan.

††††††††††††††††††††††††††

Doris grumpily answered the phone on its third ring. "Oh, 'tis you. Wait a minute, lieutenant, I'll get my husband. And you can have him...he does naught but pace since he came home, will nae tell me why, and you do nae tell me why, so you just take him and send him home when he decides to talk to me again."

"Woman, give me that. What has possessed you to speak so? Who be it? Hello?"

Despite the circumstances, Sloane smiled. Doris' quick temper was legendary, and he didn't envy anyone who was on the receiving end of it. Having been there himself, he knew better than to get involved; he was grateful that, this time, they weren't in the same room. Experiencing her bad side once in a week was more than enough for him.

"Irish, I don't have time now. I'll call when I get to the

station, but I'm taking Kent in, and he's worried about Miss LaRue being alone; something about somebody hitting her and his client being with her. Get there and I'll call in about thirty minutes with whatever I've found out."

Jimmy hung up and turned to his wife, who held her hand up to silence him. "Just go, but you best remember to come home in one piece."

He smiled and kissed her forehead before limping out to his car.

Chapter Nine
The Luck of the Irish

J IMMY TAPPED AT THE door. No answer. That wasn't a problem; he had made the cubbyhole in the molding where Lauren kept the spare key. He let himself in, but there was still no answer. The house was completely silent. "Lauren?"

No answer, and he was getting a bad feeling. There were supposed to be two people here. Somebody should have answered him.

He began searching the house, but found nothing. No Lauren, no note, no Masao. Slowly, he made his way to the second floor, then to the attic. Still nothing.

Before he could finish his search, the phone rang and Sloane told him everything, including where Kent had stashed the notebook. Although Jimmy was sure Sloane didn't know everything, at least he had more information than he did before. If only he could figure out how it helped him. From what Sloane said, it didn't sound like Lauren was in any shape to go anywhere. So where was she?

With no clues inside, Jimmy moved outside, each step harder than the last. Still, he didn't have time to nurse his aching back; he had a missing friend to find.

Finally, he found his clue. It wasn't a good sign, but it was something. The earth bore fresh scars where somebody had been dragged through the sand, leaving deep furrows. They ended next to some tire marks, refusing to tell him anything else. He followed the car as far as he could, but soon the vehicle had turned onto the paved road, and all trace of it vanished.

Now what? Sloane had warned him to stay away from the station to avoid putting himself in the crosshairs. Kent was probably going to be questioned for the rest of the night and detained for the whole 48 hours.

The best thing he could do was keep working. He had searched every crime scene except one, and according to Sloane, nobody was there.

It wasn't far to the dead woman's house. After everything that happened, he was sure a busybody like the newly departed would have been working overtime watching Kent's house. Somebody like that would have a logbook somewhere, just in case they could use it to make trouble for somebody.

The police had been thorough; he had to admit that. There was fingerprint dust everywhere, and it looked like everything helpful had already been taken to the station. But Kent was counting on him, and he was good at seeing things other people couldn't. If the police had missed anything, Jimmy was the one to find it.

So began another tedious search. Room after room was carefully documented with photo after photo and note after note, step after weary, agonizing step. Nothing stood out, but he wasn't going to quit yet. There was still a stack of papers left to comb through in her magazine stand.

As he reached for the first stack, he noticed a tiny piece of black sticking out from under the rotary phone, and he knew he had just struck gold. The lady held onto it like it was her lifeline when talking to Jimmy after the fire, and it was obviously something she wanted to keep hidden.

He slid it from under the phone and began carefully thumbing through the pages. This should clear Kent, and that was all Jimmy wanted at the moment. Any other question could wait.

Slipping the book into his jacket pocket, Jimmy froze. He knew he was alone in the house, but he had just heard a noise at the front door. There wasn't a good place to hide in the cramped room, and they'd be inside at any moment.

Quickly, Jimmy slid back through the window he had used to sneak inside. Provided he could stay silent, he could use her hedge as a hiding spot. But before he could use it to disappear, he needed to erase any sign that he had been there. That meant sliding the window shut again.

He held his breath, remembering how the window had stuck when he opened it. It had been closed for so long that the paint had nearly turned to concrete, but he had pried it loose. It had made an awful creaking sound, and if it did that again, he'd be toast.

Luck was on his side. The obstinate window closed noiselessly, and he could hear the men perfectly.

The first voice whined. "Why didn't you just get it when you whacked her?"

"By the time she quit yammering, and I finally found out everything she knew, somebody was beating on the door and I had to get lost or get pinched."

"Should we be looking for anything else?"

"Nah, just the book. She said she made notes of everything. We might even track down that shamus and Jap from it."

Jimmy kept moving closer to the window, then took a deep breath and peeked through, trying to stay behind the curtain's outline. It was foggy outside; with a little more luck, the mist would shelter him and he would remain invisible.

Now he had seen them, but he had to identify them. Sure, he could sketch them, but he had a pocket camera. He was nervous about pushing his luck, especially after relying on it so much already, but he tried anyway. He had identified the killers and found the missing evidence they wanted. Now, he needed to escape with the evidence.

The chain-link fence was an obstacle, but his crutches would make an excellent pole if he timed it right. He did, but his trousers snagged on the wire. *Glad it wasn't any higher, or I'd never have made it.*

A quick tug and he was free; another yank and his crutches were free, too. Staying hidden in the shrubs, he slipped back to his car and pulled away, headed for the darkroom at Lauren's to develop his pictures.

††††††††††††††††††††††††††

"HE'S NOT BREATHING!"

"We need him to sign. Wake him up!"

"I don't know what to do!"

††††††††††††††††††††††††††

"Wʜᴀᴛ ɪs ɢᴏɪɴɢ ᴏɴ up there?" Lauren whispered to herself, pulling to the side of the road and switching off her headlights. She leaned over the steering wheel for a better look, then saw somebody push something out of the back seat.

Not wanting to give them a chance to do any more damage, Lauren switched her lights back on and sped toward them.

†††††††††††††††††††††††††††

Tᴡᴇɴᴛʏ ᴍɪɴᴜᴛᴇs ᴇᴀʀʟɪᴇʀ, Lᴀᴜʀᴇɴ's sleep was interrupted by someone arguing. She blinked, trying to place the sound, then wobbled to the door and listened. These voices were strangers, but one of them mentioned her by name. Footsteps moved closer to her door, and she didn't have time to do anything except duck behind the secret panel in her room.

Looking through the peephole, Lauren silently uttered a prayer of thanks, remembering how close she had come to boarding up the secret passages Kent had discovered in her home. There was only one way this night could be worse, and not having a centuries-old hiding spot in the wall would be it.

From her vantage point, she could see them both. Judging by how they looked, they were probably brothers. One was tall, had an athletic build, and a cauliflower ear. Jimmy had taught her what that meant; the man was either a boxer now or had been one in the past. The other was a few inches shorter, with a flabby midsection. Both had faces that seemed to have a permanent sneer etched on them, and both were combing through her room.

Her hiding spot kept her safe. After several minutes of searching, they finally gave up, leaving her alone in the wall. She could still hear every sound around her; first, the door slammed shut, and then a car started. There wasn't time to play it safe. She needed to see what was happening, even if it turned out to be an ambush.

Tiptoeing out of the secret room, she crept toward the front door; the only sound was her shallow breaths as she willed herself to be invisible. What if somebody was still there? Would her training be enough?

It would have to be. She kept moving, looking for anybody still inside, but there was nobody. That was a good sign, so she hurried outside.

Quickly, she climbed into the waiting car. Once again, she was following somebody, but she was much less confident this time. Her last attempt had nearly resulted in her own death. This time, they were almost certain to be expecting her.

Still, when the car in front of her slowed to a stop, so

did she.

Lauren hesitated when she saw something being unceremoniously dumped out of the back seat. If she didn't stick with the car, she would lose her only lead, but the lump looked too suspicious. She couldn't leave without finding out what was inside.

The car's occupants must have panicked when they saw headlights. They peeled off with a squeal and a roar, leaving her alone in her car.

Clutching her pistol, she parked in the same place the other car had, looking for whatever had been tossed. Morning was still thirty minutes from shining its light on her mystery, and there were quite a few lumps lurking in the darkness. Most were only boulders, but one seemed different. It seemed like something—someone, maybe? The form was contorted from the fall, but it was a person.

It was too small to be Kent. Where was he? There wasn't time to worry about that now. Whoever the person was, he was obviously in trouble. He wasn't breathing and there was no pulse, but thanks to Doris, Lauren knew what to do. Without wasting a moment, she began chest compressions.

Finally, the man was breathing again. They were shallow gasps, true, but the man's chest rose and fell without her help. Now she needed to find out what was wrong with him to keep him alive.

There was something sticky on the back of his head. She felt it. When she looked at her hand, she saw it. Blood. Not surprising, but she had to stop the bleeding or the man wouldn't have a chance. And to accomplish that, she had to find the wound.

Who would have thought that would be the easiest part of her day? Not Lauren. But she easily found it, even in the dark; a huge bump that was gushing blood. She was prepared for that too, thanks to Doris, and quickly pulled out her trusty medicine kit. Not a simple task in the dark, but she managed.

Trying to get him into the car was another problem, but she used the rope from her trunk to make a harness and pulley. That made it easier, but he was still dead weight. Huffing, she cradled his head long enough it didn't bash into the metal frame, then scrambled after him. She had done everything she could for him, but he needed more, fast. Her tires squealed in protest as she hurried him to the hospital.

In twenty minutes, they were in the parking lot and she was blaring the horn. Two orderlies came scurrying out with a stretcher, and Lauren was finally rewarded with her first glimpse of the patient.

"Mr. Nagasaki!"

Although Lauren didn't know much, she told the nurse what she could. Thankfully, the nurse remembered him from the last time. What Lauren didn't know was already in his file; hopefully, that would be enough to save him. That was all she could do for him, but there was still so much to do. And at the top of her list was finding her friend.

Sloane might know something if she could reach him. It took some time, but she convinced the nurse to let her use the phone.

"Hello, Sloane here."

"Yes, Lieutenant. This is Lauren LaRue. William's friend?"

"Oh, yeah, he's out on the town again, huh?"

Lauren was puzzled. "Excuse me?"

"I know he's been gettin' in trouble a lot lately, but he'll stumble home soon enough."

Time to make a guess. "I gather you cannot talk now?"

"You got it. I'm sure he'll be able to explain everything when you see him."

Lauren hung up, confused but certain that, somehow, Sloane was telling her to get home. She couldn't go home, but she could do the next best thing.

††††††††††††††††††††††††††

"Who was that?"

Sloane chuckled. "You know how I am with names. Just can't quite put 'em together right. But her old man goes on one bender after another lately."

The officer laughed. "Reckon we oughta roust him for her?"

"Nah. Like I told her, he'll be home sooner rather than later."

††††††††††††††††††††††††††

Jimmy was working in the darkroom when he heard the phone ringing in the other room. He swore lightly under his breath before catching himself; some habits were harder to break than others, no matter how angry it made his wife.

"Hello?"

"Jimmy?" Lauren's voice was quivering and incredulous.

"Ah, cailín! Glad to hear from ye. Boss was worried about ye, and when I got here, ye were gone."

"Yes, well, I'm at the hospital with Mr. Nagasaki. I do not know what happened to him, but I heard two men arguing and took refuge. They came searching for me, but when they couldn't find me, they left with Mr. Nagasaki. I brought him to the hospital, but he is not doing well at all, Jimmy. I don't know what they did, but he is doing quite badly. And what is worse, I think they have William. He was gone when I came out, and he would never have left his post voluntarily."

"Well, certain sure and ye are right about that last part. He's been hauled off to the hoosegow. Sloane is keeping it close to his vest, but has been trying to keep me posted on everything."

"He was arrested???"

"Yes, mo páiste, for the murder of the lads who tried to murder him, and that of the angry banshee who lived across from him. I've been developing me film from the different crime scenes and looking through her notes, but I'll be with ye in two shakes of a lamb's tail. Keep alert—they'll probably try to come take him again if they find out he still be living."

"I understand, Jimmy. I will see to his safety. You keep yourself safe, all right?"

"Surely, páiste. Ye as well. See ye soon."

Lauren immediately found herself an inconspicuous seat where she could watch the hospital entrance and the door to Masao's room. She ignored the magazine in her hands; it kept her face shielded and her hands busy, but that was its only purpose. Her eyes constantly watched for trouble, and her mind was miles away.

What evidence could possibly convince the police that William Kent, who spent his time risking life and limb for strangers, was going on a killing spree?

†††††††††††††††††††††††††††

It took almost an hour, but Jimmy finished developing and organizing the pictures before showing them to Lauren at the hospital. He didn't know much about the case against their friend, but what he knew helped explain the images she was looking at. She found new ways to impress him, and this was no exception; not even the pictures of the dead teens broke her focus, and together the pair began searching for the answers that would clear Kent.

Lauren paused when she saw the two men Jimmy had spotted that morning. "I am almost positive that this is the man who was talking to Mrs. Nagasaki at the swamp house—the one who chased me through the woods."

"Great! Now we only need to give the cladhaire a name, and we'll have them."

"How do you usually do that?"

"Nope, can't do it that way. Usually, we get Sloane or Johnstone for a helping hand. The last time I did that, it led me to the bodies of the eight lads what tried to kill Boss. Any lead I get this time, he'd look into first—assuming his bull-headed associates even let him check it out to begin with. Coppers aren't usually known for being open-minded."

"What, then?"

"I'll ask Mrs. Watanabe if she recognizes him. Other than that, I'll try matching it to any photographs I can find about the attacks or the new landowners.

"Are ye all right?"

The abrupt shift in conversation surprised Lauren, and she set the pictures down to study Jimmy. Instead of speaking, he pointed at her neck, and she realized her mistake. She had been fidgeting with the scarf during their entire conversation, subconsciously drawing his attention to the rope burns around her neck even as she hoped to hide them. There was no way she was going to admit that she had nearly let somebody hang her, and she clenched her jaw firmly.

Realizing he wasn't going to get an answer, Jimmy deftly removed the scarf, revealing the raw marks that encircled her neck.

"Begorrah, cailín! What have ye gone and done to yourself?"

Lauren snatched the scarf out of his hands, quickly tying it back around her neck. "It was touch and go for a while, but you taught me how to handle the situation, so I did. I am only slightly the worse for wear, so I would thank you to keep this between us."

Jimmy nodded and changed the subject. "Look, we're going to have to divide and conquer. I doubt anyone will find him here, but he has nobody else to watch over him, so I hereby dub ye his guardian angel. If the scallywags come looking for him, best ye be here waiting for them, since ye have the best idea who it is will be coming."

"So, you trust me on my own? Even after I nearly got myself killed?"

Jimmy's eyes twinkled mischievously. "Why? Do ye think I should not?"

"No—no, I can do it. You just surprised me. William would have sent me to bed until I turned eighty."

He only smiled as he walked out, planning to meet with Mrs. Watanabe. If she was half as curious as Kent's dead neighbor, she should recognize one of them.

"No, I do not know these men."

Although disappointed, Jimmy wasn't surprised. The crew had been so careful. Why would they slip up now and give him a name?

Oh well, he had a backup idea. Out came the list of names—anybody who had purchased the properties since the attacks had begun. That was another disappointment, so he thanked her and left. Hopefully, his next line of investigation would be more productive.

At least he had thought to get the addresses of every name he had found, from the family of the dead kids to the people who had bought the properties. He drove to the first house and knocked on the door. Nothing. So, he moved on to the second house, then the third, then the fourth. Still no luck, and he headed to the fifth house.

After so many disappointments, he finally had a match! The man who answered the door was the same one who purchased the house next to Masao Nagasaki.

The man's voice was as surly as his appearance. "What do you want?"

"Excuse me, sir, but I'm an investigator who was hired to find an Otto van Richter?"

"Regarding what, exactly?"

"That's a private matter, I'm afraid. Unless ye be he, I cannot tell me client's business to every Tom, Dick, and Harry."

"We are at an impasse, then, because what kind of fool would I be to tell any Tom, Dick, or Harry where to find somebody?"

"A helpful one?" Jimmy offered a winsome smile, hoping to wiggle some information out of the man.

"Helpful, bah."

"Well, say we meet in the middle, then. I was hired by

the man's family, hoping to get in touch with him."

The man opened the door and stepped outside. "I have no family,"

"So, ye are van Richter?"

"Yes, but what is that to you? As I have already mentioned, I am without any relatives."

"Technically, 'tis true enough, as 'twas the estate that hired me. If ye could prove ye are the right man?"

"What do you mean? You found me. Isn't that proof enough?"

Jimmy nodded apologetically. "But ye see, sir, I've had four clients claiming to be me man. Money tends to do that to people. But of course, if ye would prefer your privacy, I can understand..."

"Wait, I did not say that. What's the name of the dead man?"

"Sigmund; if ye be the right man, he be your uncle. And ye have not seen him in years, but are the only remaining family. Do ye think ye can remember the rest of his name? Just to prove ye are who ye say, and save us both some time?"

"An Uncle...Sigmund, you say?"

"Yes, sir."

"It seems like I do remember an Uncle Sigmund...Baker, perhaps?"

"No, sorry. It seems I have wasted your time and mine."

"No—it has been so long, such a very long time—could it be Bauer? Yes, that is it. Sigmund Bauer."

One name on Jimmy's list was Sigfried Baer. Not an exact match, but close enough to be a possible alias. Obviously, this man had also been testing him. Maybe, with a little of the luck of the Irish, he could get more. "The man I'm looking for has been here for years. The first fella I spoke with fudged it. Not to be rude, but I notice you've still got a pretty noticeable accent there."

"Ya, so do you. How long since you were a mick?"

Jimmy forced himself to stay calm. "Now, don't get sore, mister. I don't have to prove who I am, but if ye want the inheritance, ye do. No skin off my nose either way."

"Of course. Mein family has been here for nearly twenty years."

He shifted his weight from one foot to the other and glanced aside uneasily, but Jimmy pretended not to notice. "Well, as far as I can tell, ye be the right fella, but ye do understand I'll need to check me facts to be sure."

Jimmy left then, pretending that he couldn't feel the man's eyes boring into his back and fighting the urge to drop him. After the man's attitude, the detective felt justified. Besides, the way van Richter stared after him left him feeling uneasy, like a rifle sight was trained on the back of his skull.

Of course, he couldn't do that—the cowardice of attacking somebody unprovoked was enough to stop him. Besides, a missing little girl was depending on his ability to keep his temper in check. So he limped back to his car, trying to look as harmless as possible before driving away.

After two blocks, he circled back and began watching the house. Now that he knew how the names were chosen, he wanted to see if he could find another alias on the list.

Two hours later, a car pulled up and honked the horn. Otto came running over, but the reunion was far from a happy one. Whoever was in the car soon had the man shouting angrily, and a moment later a shot rang out.

Otto fell to the ground while Jimmy fussed with the ignition. Now that he needed the car to start, it had cooled enough to refuse, and sputtered lazily at his efforts. The other driver had no such problems; his car had never been turned off, and he sped away, leaving the man in a pool of crimson.

Finally, Jimmy's car started, and he roared after the shooter, planning to stop for nothing. And if he hadn't seen movement from the fallen man, he wouldn't have. His foot hesitated to brake—he might be following the little girl's last chance to get home safely instead of in a coffin. He had no way of knowing how badly injured the man was—what if he died, and Jimmy had let the other man get away? Besides, would it really be so bad if the man died? Anybody who wanted to make their living bullying those weaker than them deserved what they got, and the fact that the man had gotten shot seemed proof enough of his involvement. Still, he could be innocent.

Jimmy had hesitated long enough that the other car was almost out of sight. He couldn't possibly catch them without revealing himself, so he skidded to a stop next to the injured man. He stretched until he could reach the passenger door, then roughly dragged him onto the seat and headed for the hospital.

As Jimmy turned into the parking lot, the man was just starting to come around. He wasn't feeling particularly charitable toward the man. Whether or not he was a Nazi, the accent left him uneasy. Add to that the nefarious things he was connected to—terrorizing the children of his former allies—and Jimmy was seriously debating shoving the man out on the hospital stoop. Why waste any more time on the man? He was close enough to help. Otto could fend for himself.

In the end, Jimmy waited until the orderlies came scurrying out with a stretcher. Van Richter had not been proven guilty of anything. If the man was guilty, he was Jimmy's best shot to find little Suki. If it wasn't for his own daughter, that probably wouldn't have warranted the extra effort, or anything other than righteous indignation, but his little girl was his light. Anyone who could hurt a child was the lowest form of life he could imagine.

As the orderlies wheeled the man inside, a sudden rap on the window brought Jimmy back to the present.

"Before y'all started working in this city, we never had to worry about collecting our patients from the parking lot. We never had anyone blow their horn for service like this is a filling station, come to think of it. Well, we had one, but she gave birth in the doorway. But now, whenever we hear a car horn, we know to expect the worst. So, who's this one?"

"Nobody nice, but I'm not sure of any more than that." Prompted by the nurse's sudden appearance, Jimmy grabbed his crutches and walked inside with her. "Admit it, life be more interesting for ye with us in it. Never a dull moment, right?"

The nurse only shook her head in response.

After a few minutes, Jimmy sweet-talked her into letting him use the phone, and he soon had Sloane on the other end of the line.

"If you keep tying one on, your old lady's liable to change the locks on you,"

"Sure and ye must've taken a harder knock than ye let on when that oaf tried to turn your lights out for good."

"Now, you know I'm at work. I can't keep playing marriage counselor to the two of you."

"Still on a short leash, eh? I think ye could have done better than making me the villain of your story, though."

"Well, I get to have a little fun, the grief you put me through. I've got business keeping me here another six hours, then I'll be off the clock and best not be disturbed."

"Don't ye be worrying about me fouling up your day off, copper. I thought ye might want an update, though..."

A shrill scream tore through the quiet hospital; Jimmy dropped the phone and hurried toward the sound.

It took only a moment to get to the source of the cry. One of the candy stripers had been sent to track down the doctor assigned to triage. Little did she know that her search for the missing man would lead to an unsettling revelation; on the floor, lying next to the bloody gurney where Otto van Richter had been, was the surgeon. Now she was sobbing uncontrollably, unable to tell Jimmy anything about what she had seen.

Jimmy heard a slight thudding sound and charged into the room across the hall, motioning Lauren to stay at her post. The window was wide open—the fugitive must have gone that way. He wriggled out the window, using his crutches to absorb the impact of his fall. It worked slightly, but the pain was still enough to cause the world to spin into blinding white. As he stood there trying to steady himself, a second pain radiated through his skull, sending him to the ground in an unconscious heap, unaware of the warning Lauren had tried to give.

Chapter Ten
An Ambush

When she saw Jimmy fall, Lauren jumped after him, calling for a nurse. She landed nimbly on one knee, pausing just long enough to check his pulse before racing after the fleeing figure.

The man was almost gone. She could hear an engine struggling to start and raced back to Jimmy's car, hoping it wouldn't have cooled enough to act temperamental.

Both cars turned over at the same time. Careful to keep her distance, Lauren followed as the man made turn after turn, trying in vain to lose any tail he might have.

Finally, he parked and headed into a small shack. Lauren followed cautiously. She needn't have bothered; the shouting coming from inside masked any sound she made. Peering through the window, she saw Mrs. Nagasaki and Otto yelling at each other, and the man was waving his pistol furiously.

Taking a deep breath, Lauren looked for the best way to sneak inside. With one body on her conscience already, she hoped to avoid any further bloodshed.

As she studied the front of the building, she noticed a doggy door, just big enough for her to squeeze through. It looked like they were in a different room; maybe they couldn't see the front door from where they were. If they couldn't, maybe she could surprise them.

One. Two. Three. Lauren counted as she tried to steady her nerves before wiggling through. The fight was still going strong; she had her advantage. Silently, she crept up behind the man before bringing the pistol butt down on his head. Before he had hit the floor, she had it trained on Misa Nagasaki.

"Thank goodness you come. He going to kill me."

Once again Lauren shifted into her Hepburn persona. "Save it. I wouldn't mind doing that myself after the trouble you've caused. Get him up and let's go."

"B-but, he too big! How I carry him?"

"I've helped bigger than him. You'll figure it out."

The pistol in her hand left her prisoner with no choice. Misa grudgingly bound the man's hands, then stumbled under his weight as they moved to Jimmy's car.

Once he was safely secured in the trunk, Lauren used

her scarf to tie Misa's hands before putting her in the back seat. "Try anything and you go in the trunk with him," Lauren warned.

The drive back to the hospital was much quicker; what had taken an hour took only thirty minutes without all the extra turns. Soon, she was honking for help. "Go get security. I brought back the man who attacked your doctor."

The night watchman wasted no time; he soon had the man securely fastened to a stretcher.

Now that he was out of the way, Lauren helped Misa out and walked her inside, then called Sloane and convinced him to come to the hospital. A nurse showed her a supply closet, and she stashed the angry woman inside to wait for the lieutenant.

Once Misa was tucked away, Lauren asked for Jimmy. When she found him watching over Masao, she almost cried with relief.

"What were you thinking? Jumping out of a window. I ought to call Doris on you right now. Are you all right? How is your head?"

"Whoa, me little cailín! 'Tis too many questions ye be asking me at one time. I be just fine, aside from a fierce pounding in me head and a sharp twinge in me back. I'll not be leaping out any more windows, and ye can take that to the bank."

His words were still sluggish. Any relief Lauren had felt was gone as she realized how weak he still was, and she helped him adjust his pillows to get more comfortable before heading to the nurses' station to intercept Sloane.

It wasn't long before the policeman walked in, Kent handcuffed to his wrist. Lauren's face turned purple as she sputtered, searching for the right words, but Sloane held his hand to silence her before she could speak. "Now take it easy, technically he's still in custody. There's a few hours before they have to turn him loose. I had to do something to convince them to let me bring him."

Kent chuckled wryly. "You know good and well you've been wanting to do this since the first time we met."

"I didn't say I hadn't," Sloane laughed. "That's just the icing on the cake. Now, ma'am, you said you had the real killer?"

"At the very least, he's involved."

"This have anything to do with that scuffle earlier?"

Lauren quickly filled them in. "Jimmy will have to tell you everything else. He never had a chance to tell me what led him to the man."

Sloane looked at the nurse. "Why didn't you call this in?"

"Mr. O'Sullivan convinced me not to. Frankly, it wasn't that difficult a decision. When y'all came for Mr. Kent, you dragged him away like the Gestapo. You should be ashamed, treating a sick man so."

Lauren nodded in agreement, while Sloane threw up his hands in surrender. "I didn't—I brought him back!"

"Potato, potat-oh. They were your colleagues. You'll be happy to know that poor Doctor Boggs will be just fine."

She pointed loftily toward Jimmy's post.

"Boss!" Jimmy happily began to struggle to his feet.

Kent motioned him to sit back down. "Stay there, you're fine,"

Jimmy sank back onto his cushioned seat wearily, and the four took turns comparing notes. Once they finished, Sloane and Kent retrieved Misa from her makeshift cell.

Misa blinked at the sudden brightness, then pointed accusingly at Lauren. "She crazy lady! Take me prisoner here! She have no right!"

"She might not, but I do." Sloane flashed his badge, and she paled. "Want to tell me what this is about?"

"I just try to protect my family."

"What of your husband? Is he not your family?" Lauren couldn't hide her contempt for the little woman.

"He old enough to protect himself. He abandon us."

Now it was Kent's turn to be shocked. "How do you figure that?"

"He make us stay where we not welcome. All this happen because of him. Now my daughter gone because he too stubborn to say he wrong."

"See here, lady, he swallowed his pride to hire me. Do you think it was easy for him to do that? To accept help from the enemy? But he needed to help his family, so here we are."

"I just want go home with my children,"

"Your home is a pile of ash," Kent said flatly.

"That not my home! That my prison. I glad it gone! I tell him, how many time I tell him, take me home. My children becoming like you joes, especially my daughter. I want them to know their ancestors. He say it not safe. It been thirteen years, no more bombs. It not safe here! But he not listen. No, not Masao Nagasaki. He must have his way, always. Where that leave us?"

The bitterness in her voice was unmistakable.

"You set him up," Kent whispered. "That's why you wanted me off the case so bad. So he wouldn't have any choice but to sell."

"I hope he sell, but whatever it take. Then you give him hope, so he stay. This all your fault. If you quit when I ask, everything fine and everybody happy. My family in Japan, not bother you anymore."

"When'd you decide your husband was expendable?"

"Do not judge me! He willing to sacrifice my children for his honor. I not."

"How long?" Kent was determined to get the truth from the woman. He was trying to hide his disgust, but knew he was failing. What's more, he didn't really care. He had his own heartbreak, and all he could see when he looked at Misa was his callous ex-wife, who had annulled their marriage as soon as he had shipped out.

Misa's defiance withered under his intense stare. "He did this," she whispered. Seeing Kent's expression, she quickly continued. "When he say he pay you, I call them. They say they help us get home. What you do?"

"Not destroy my family."

"I forgot." Misa's contemptuous tone returned. "You American, have no idea what it like to be me. We hated here!"

"And your attitude ain't helped. Did you ever even try to be part of your new country, to make it home? Or did you think we'd roll out the red carpet for someone who not so long ago tried to destroy us? Yeah, you mighta got a raw deal—but trust is earned. Everybody ain't going to hate you forever, but you acted exactly the way they expected you to. You proved 'em right."

"You know nothing!"

"I know what it's like to be a prisoner to <u>your</u> countrymen. You think this is bad, you shoulda tried a cruise on a hell ship. This country ain't perfect, and people get judged for rotten reasons every day. But it still took you in despite your past and gave you a chance to make a life."

"Some life! It not easy choice to sacrifice him, but you both made choice for me. I not going to apologize for keeping my children safe. I tell the men what to do, and they do it. Then you come along and stop it, they get mad at me. Say I fail. So I must make right. I try ask you nice, but you won't listen, so I put poison on your doorknob. I made medicine back home, I know how to do it, it easy for me. Or maybe not so easy, since you still here. I never work with giant before, so I guess. Must have guessed wrong. I say I took care of you, so they go to scare him, tell him you dead, and sell before somebody else die. But you still help him, so I came up with idea of using Suki—she only one convince him change his mind. But when you keep helping, they take her for real. Now I just try to get her, take my family home. I sell my jewelry to pay, who need house?"

"Lady, you realize you ain't goin' anywhere, right? You're up to your neck in this."

Misa blinked. Obviously, the thought had never occurred to her that she was doing anything wrong, and she definitely had never imagined that she would be held accountable for it. "I just want go home! Please, you never see me or kids again. Everything I did, I did for them. What so bad about that?"

Kent glared at her. "You tried to kill me and your husband both. You got your daughter kidnapped. That's what's so wrong!"

Sloane cleared his throat. "This is great and all, but it doesn't clear you," he whispered to Kent.

"I know. Hopefully, Jimmy and my gal Friday can do that." Kent pulled Lauren to him and affectionately kissed her head. "You did good, kid. Mighty good."

Lauren blushed as the nurse came toward them. "I thought you might be interested to know that your ruffian is awake and talking."

After a brief discussion, Jimmy opted to stay with Masao and Lauren with Misa. Kent and Sloane left to question Otto.

They found the man sullen and trying to free himself

from the restraints. "I have nothing to say."

"That's fine, you just listen. We got you cold on the attempted murder of Misa Nagasaki, Masao Nagasaki, and James O'Sullivan. Also, the murders of Wally King, Eddie Haskell, Will Brent, Frankie Long, Al Newsome, Jack Thomson, Jim Morrissey, and Teddy Peters." Sloane looked up from his pad for a moment before continuing. "You followed them home from Kent's house and finished them off instead of paying them for their work—or maybe you were worried they'd talk. You've been scaring people away from one particular section of town. Wonder why that is? It has nothing to do with the Klan. That's just your cover. You want the land. Yup, that's gotta be it."

The man grimaced but remained silent.

"Man like you, your blade is part of you." Kent stroked his chin thoughtfully. "You wouldn't be caught dead without it, if you'll pardon the expression. Lauren would've found it. So where'd you hide it?"

Kent began searching the clothes on the table, watching for any sign from the man that he was getting close. And when he got to the belt, he finally got it. "Lieutenant, I ain't going to get my prints on it, but I'd bet my life there's a murder weapon in that buckle."

Sloane smiled. "Which means we have means. Now

we've got evidence."

Seeing the man open his mouth, Sloane hurriedly silenced him. "No, you don't wanna say anything to make yourself look more guilty. You have the right to stay quiet and wait for your lawyer to advise you to say somebody planted the murder weapon in your custom-made belt. Stay quiet—I'd hate to have to offer you a deal. Everything we've got on you, you probably couldn't offer much, anyway. Guys like you go straight to the chair, and I'll sleep just fine knowing that.

"Say, you ever seen anybody get the chair?" Sloane asked Kent. When Kent said no, he went into detail before turning to the man. "Hope it was worth it."

"Wait! What if I give you the name of the man who hired me?"

"I said not to do that. You've got a right to hope a jury lets you off, and I have the right to look forward to seeing you get strapped into that chair before riding the electric highway. I bet those restraints won't be much different from the ones you've got on now."

"See here, I want to talk! He paid me five hundred dollars to scare those people, and paid the others too. Those kids—they did their part, then got big heads and threatened to go to the authorities and say everything they knew. I don't know how they imagined their threats would end, but I was not surprised when he shut them up."

"What's this puppet master's name?"

"I do not know that."

Sloane started back to the door, and the man called after him in a panicked voice. "Honestly, I have no idea. I am to call him from a payphone, and when I finish, I'm supposed to call again. He's waiting for my call now, to determine whether I finally got the Nagasaki land."

Sloane borrowed a dictaphone and recorded the confessions of both criminals, then dialed the number Otto gave him. After holding the receiver to the thug's ear, he waited until the man finished talking before calling the nurse. "Can I take him now?"

"Medically, no. We need to keep him under observation for a few more hours. After all, he has lost consciousness twice in a very short amount of time. I'll admit I'd rather not keep him here any longer than I have to. Not after what he did the last time we tried to help him. If you wait another two hours, and he hasn't taken a turn for the worse, you may do what you want with him."

Sloane telephoned Detective Johnstone, requesting that the young policeman bring his partner and stand guard over the prisoner while he was at the hospital.

While waiting, the man admitted to knowing about the murder of Kent's busybody neighbor and confessed to his role in the real estate scam.

He posed as different buyers using names his employer provided. The man wasn't German; he was a talented voice actor paid to be whoever his employer demanded. The 'boss' told him only what he needed to know to create his characters. When Jimmy mentioned an inheritance, he remembered how the boss chose the aliases, and used that to guess what name would get him the money.

'Otto'—whose real name was Ned Jones—knew nothing else, except that his boss wanted all the land. He would only know the next step once the man purchased the remaining two lots.

It felt much longer, but Johnstone arrived in only fifteen minutes, leaving Sloane free to clear Kent. And with Sloane driving, it took only a few minutes to arrive at the police station, where they marched straight to the office of Sloane's superior.

Although the captain's face was purple with rage, he agreed grudgingly that Kent was innocent and released him.

Sloane waited for Kent to leave, then leaned closer to the captain. "Can we talk somewhere private?"

"Yeah, it's past time for a man-to-man talk."

The captain walked into the empty cellblock and closed the door behind him before leading Sloane to the end cell. "What do you mean, embarrassin' me like that?"

Sloane glared at the captain. "From what that man confessed to, the community has been terrorized. Yet I haven't heard about it. Something like that would've been reported to you, Tim. You must've squashed it. So, either you're involved, don't want bad press, or you want to be rid of that community as much as the gangsters tearing it apart. I'm pretty sure you're not involved; you like power, not money, and I haven't seen any evidence of extra cash. But you're a self-righteous bigot and always have been. Time to man up and do the right thing."

"Are you threatening me?!?" The man's fat face contorted with anger as he glowered at Sloane.

"Stating a fact. You're a policeman. Time to act like it."

Sloane started toward the door, but the captain wasn't finished. Blinded with rage, he moved before Sloane could take a step, propelling the lieutenant face-first into the iron cell bars. He tried to steady himself, but an explosion of light dropped him to the floor.

††††††††††††††††††††††††

KENT WAITED UNTIL HE was out of the station and around the corner to look at the note Sloane had slipped him. His eyes wide, he raced to the nearest payphone.

A woman was already inside the booth. He knocked on the glass—politely at first, then with increasing urgency as he pleaded for her to let him use the phone for only a minute. It was no use; she merely looked at him in annoyance. After standing there a few moments longer, he decided he could run faster than she could talk.

Each step made his breathing harder. His lungs burned from the effort and his vision blurred, but he was almost at his destination. Finally, he reached it: it was in sight, now he was through the door. "I've got-the-the scoop of-of a lifetime. Get your-your camera and let's-let's go."

"Wait just a minute, sir. How do I know this isn't just a prank?"

Kent rolled his eyes as he steadied himself against the wall. *Sure. I nearly killed myself to josh a stranger.* He handed her the note before he spoke again. "Lieutenant Robert Sloane passed me this maybe, maybe fifteen minutes ago?" His breathing was still sharp and jagged, but at least the world wasn't spinning as much. "Sloane says the police have been covering up multiple murders, and he's going to prove it, but we need to get there fast."

"We'll take my car. Come on, Perry." The reporter grabbed her photographer and led the way to her '53 Riviera. "Sorry, it's gonna be a tight squeeze for you, big boy."

It took only a few minutes to get back to the station, but it was enough to let Kent catch his breath. Adrenaline surged through him as he charged through the door. "Where's the captain?" he roared.

The clicking of typewriter keys and the hum of voices stopped, and a hush fell over the busy room. Every head turned to him, then all present jumped when a phone rang, shattering the uneasy silence. A chorus of nervous gulps sounded through the room. One man nodded slightly toward the captain's office door, which flew open with a bang as its scowling occupant emerged.

Seeing Kent, the scowl deepened. "Get out before I lock you up!"

Kent closed the space between them in only three steps, towering menacingly over the shorter man. "You had your shot already. Where's Sloane?"

The captain blinked, temporarily blinded by a flash from the photographer's bulb. "Nobody invited the press, and you blasted newshawks can get fodder somewhere else. There's nothing for you here."

Kent ignored the man's efforts to block him, pushing past and shouting again. "Sloane!"

Seeing his friend was nowhere in sight, he turned to face the weasel in charge. "Where is he?"

Even the bull-headed captain knew enough to step back from the raw anger oozing from the detective. "I don't know. He stormed out not long after you left. You make more problems for me than anything else in this town."

Growling with exasperation, Kent turned back to the room. "Who saw Sloane last? What was his last known position?"

A patrolman hesitantly pointed at the captain. "They went to the cells together, but Sloane didn't come out."

There was a murmur around the room as everyone timidly agreed with him. Kent angrily shoved the captain aside before forcing his way into the cell block. "Sloane, you here? Answer me!"

Silence...

More silence.

The captain sneered at Kent. "What did you expect to find?"

Another blinding flash. Kent blinked and wiped his

eyes, then began searching again, the reporter and photographer hot on his heels.

Kent motioned to the reporter.

She kneeled for a closer look. "Is that blood?"

Kent nodded and followed the trail to a stack of boxes. Although dust covered the floor, something had obviously disturbed it in that corner. He easily slid the boxes out of the way, revealing an old wooden door with iron bars. The rusty black was sporting a dull silver band that looked suspiciously like a cuff, and Kent began shoving the old door until it finally slid open.

The blinding light of the photographer's bulb punctuated every moment as Kent forced his way into the tiny old room. A dull shuffling sound mingled with the creaking of the door as something was dragged along with the ancient oak. Although the detective never looked away from the captain, he had a sinking feeling that the 'something' was his friend.

After several inches, Kent glimpsed Sloane's boots dragging limply across the floor, then moved inside to find his friend's motionless body hanging from the door, suspended by the handcuff around his wrist.

"Give me the keys!" Kent thundered, once again towering over the trembling captain.

Rivers of sweat poured off the man's brow as he

fumbled with the keys, his face white with terror. "I—I don't know what happened," the man said lamely.

Kent didn't wait to hear another lie. He lifted the shivering man and body-slammed him into the wall, ripped the keys from his hand, and flung him into the boxes. "I'll deal with you later. Right now there's someone much more important to tend to."

The reporter moved to support Sloane, while several officers grabbed the disgraced captain as he tried to scamper away. Before Kent could remove the cuffs, the photographer started to take a photo, only to be blocked by the detective. "I don't want this to be what people think of when they see him."

"It could help in court..."

Kent wasn't hearing it. He wasn't even sure if his friend was alive, but he wasn't wasting time posing for a picture. There was still a chance Sloane was alive under all that blood and duct tape. Although he couldn't stop the pictures, he didn't wait for them either. He quickly released the cuff before gently lowering the lieutenant to the floor.

That was the easy part. Taking the tape off Sloane's face would be much harder, but it had to be responsible for his weak breathing. His nostrils were almost completely covered, and his mouth was taped shut.

There was no way to do this gently. Best to rip it off quickly and get it over with, then pray that would be enough to let the policeman breathe again.

Several forceful tugs later, Kent had torn the tape away, leaving angry red welts and ripping massive chunks of hair from the back of the policeman's head. A strained gurgle, then a gasp and cough; Sloane began breathing freely again. After several more ragged breaths, his chest finally began a rhythmic pattern, and Kent moved to the tape holding Sloane's other arm stiffly to his side. When that fell away, his breathing should go back to normal. Should.

With nothing else to do now that Sloane was on the ground, the reporter was furiously scribbling notes, occasionally glancing around to see the reactions of the people around her. The tall stranger had been right. He had handed her the scoop of a lifetime, and she couldn't wait to get it on the front page.

The worried detective ignored her, still focused on his friend. Now that he was free, Kent carried Sloane to his Police Pursuit and peeled off to the hospital.

As the orderlies wheeled Sloane away, Kent staggered off to find Jimmy. The adrenaline was wearing off, and he was finally feeling the exhaustion.

"Boss? What be ye doing here?"

Kent collapsed into his friend's empty chair before explaining what had happened.

Jimmy listened closely before something suddenly clicked. "Boss, I should've realized it. I'm as glaikit as me woman says..."

Setting his notepad on the table, Jimmy began writing initials and then rearranging them, shielding it until he was ready.

"Look familiar?"

Kent stared at the name, trying to place it, but finally shook his head.

Jimmy scribbled a few more things. "Now?"

The two exchanged glances before hurrying to the police detectives, still standing guard over Jones. No matter how much Kent wanted to get back to work, he couldn't leave Masao unguarded. Plus, he still needed to give his statement, explaining what had happened at the station. He had to make time to speak with the two men; once he finished, he asked them to split up, and Johnstone agreed.

Finally, the pair could start working again. Neither could move quickly, but they did their best. Soon, using Jimmy's car, they were headed to a local realtor's office.

"Do we go in and rattle him, see where he runs when he's scared?"

Kent shook his head. "Too risky. He might just as easily call whoever's holding Suki and have them get rid of her. Time's on our side, not his. He's waiting to make the swap, Suki for the deed."

"And we still need to find out why."

"At this point, I don't even care why. We know who. Let's figure out where and leave the why to somebody who does care. I'm ready to be done with this case."

Eventually, it was closing time. A man walked out, and Jimmy nudged his friend. "Does that look like Lauren's ferret face to ye?"

Kent nodded. When the man drove away, they were ready, and although they knew he would likely be paranoid, they hoped Jimmy's car was inconspicuous enough to blend in.

Another long drive followed. There were several stops, but all of them were too quick to warrant more than a little notation to come investigate them later. Each seemed unimportant until the man stopped in a field and flashed his headlights.

This had to be it. The flashing lights were an obvious signal, and all the two detectives needed was to find out who answered it.

Nothing. Several minutes passed; still nothing. Then the man abruptly started his car and doubled back, leaving his pursuers baffled.

With no time to do anything else, Jimmy stated his plan. "I'll get out and look around. Ye follow him, and either come get me in two hours or send Lauren after me."

"Be careful."

Kent waited only long enough for Jimmy to disappear into the bush before following the vanishing taillights into the night. In case the strange events had been a test, Kent stayed back even farther. There was almost no traffic, but William Kent was confident in his abilities.

Finally, the car stopped. Unlike the many other stops, the car was switched off this time. That was different, so Kent did the same before following the retreating figure into the darkness.

Although the path they followed was overgrown, it was visible, especially under the light of the waning moon. Unfortunately, the light wasn't enough to illuminate all the brambles and blackberry vines. Each snagged at Kent's trousers as he moved, but it did nothing more than slow the dogged detective. He kept his prey in sight; even though the suspect seemed more familiar with the trail, he stumbled too.

After several minutes, an abandoned house came into view. Kent was only a few feet behind his target, but the man had already disappeared into the house and was talking to someone. Listening by the broken window, the detective was surprised to overhear his name. He was even more surprised to learn the man was leaving a message with the night answering service for the Kent Detective Agency.

"Make sure he knows I've got the kid. Tell him to meet me with the deed at the old Parsons place or she buys the farm."

Kent knew he couldn't risk waiting another second. Morning was near. He was almost certain the little girl was hidden somewhere nearby, and the villain's words worried him. Suki was running out of time, and he was not leaving her at the mercy of this menace. So, even though he couldn't see through the dirty glass, he hurried inside. Too easy usually meant a trap, but he didn't have time to be thorough. All he could do was look behind each door as he slipped noiselessly from one room to the next, each one disappointingly sparse.

Suddenly, he saw the man in a room at the end of the hallway, his gun pressed against the little girl's head, using the tiny figure as his personal shield.

Kent wished Jimmy was there in his place. Jimmy was the marksman. Sure, Kent was good, but there was no room for error. There was so little of the man visible behind Suki that the slightest miscalculation would end in her death, not his. He could only watch as the realtor rubbed the barrel on her dirty cheek; his head felt like it would explode. His hand was shaking; he had to steady himself if he was going to help the little girl. His chance would come. Now he needed to breathe and wait for it.

There—his shot. A car door slammed in the distance, and the crook stretched to look out the window. Kent fired, and glass exploded everywhere.

He blinked in surprise and pivoted. How had he fallen for such a dumb trick? But he had. And now, instead of freeing Suki, he had alerted her captor to his presence. There were only two options left; either become invisible and try to sneak up on his prey, or lure his quarry out for a clear shot. Whichever plan he used, he needed to make his choice fast.

Before he could decide, he heard Suki whimper. She wasn't far away. It sounded like only a wall separated them, but there was no door to the sound. It was time to go to the next room, and hope the door was there. He would have to be extra careful now that he had announced himself, but for the sake of the tiny young girl, he'd have to risk it.

The next room was also empty and easily cleared.

There was another door, and it had to be the one she was being held in. It was in the right place, but the door was closed now. The man had probably shut it as soon as Kent fired the shot.

Remembering Misa's trick, Kent tugged his glove, just to be safe. It was securely in its place, so he flung open the door.

As the flimsy door swung open, Kent felt a sharp sting. *Not again. Please, God. Not now.* Despite his caution, he had walked into an ambush again. He stumbled into the room toward Suki, sitting as still as a statue. He was too close to give up, to let his body stop for the rest that it was demanding, so he forced himself to keep going until he finally reached her. "I—I got you, kid." He tried desperately to pick her up. Instead, he fell to the floor, her tiny hand clutching his.

†††††††††††††††††††††††††††

KENT WOKE UP SLOWLY, everything around him fuzzy. He forced his eyes open but felt too heavy to do anything else. What happened? He couldn't remember, and for a moment, he was too groggy to care. A soft whimper quickly caught his attention. Fighting to focus, everything was still too blurry to see.

"Well, you finally woke up. It's about time. I was getting bored. This just isn't fun without you."

A sudden pain broke through the fog, and Kent spit out a mouthful of blood as he tried to understand what was happening.

"That's better, but still a way to go." The voice echoed in Kent's head, confusing him even more as a second pain radiated through his skull. Whose voice was it?

The next blow landed in his chest, leaving him gasping for air and still completely bewildered. A little girl sat on a decaying mattress in the corner of the room, watching. Something was wrong with her. He could see it in her terrified little eyes. Something was off. She was too calm for her age, too unnaturally still, and there was not enough life in her eyes. Yet despite her ailment, the little girl never looked away from him, and even seemed more aware of what was happening than he was. Every blow sent a shudder through her tiny frame, but she still refused to look away. He kept trying to tell her not to watch; his mouth couldn't form the words. He finally gave up and began squeezing his eyes shut tight, hoping against hope that she would copy him. She refused.

Why was she shivering? The air was hot. It was always hot there. And he had never seen a child imprisoned in the camps, let alone one of their own. Why had the Imperials captured her? Somehow, he had to help her, to get her far away from such a terrible place.

Another blow left his head spinning. He focused on the pain—it gave him something to hold on to. As long as he could feel the blows, he wasn't dead yet.

The short little man turned to the terrified child as he spoke to Kent. "I need her for a little longer. You, not so much. I just need you to give her father a message, and just too bad for you that you don't need to be alive to give it. This message works best given by a dead man, and the more you suffer first, the more effective it is. I'll drop you off with one of her fingers—which would you want to live without?"

There was no force on earth strong enough to restrain Kent after that. While the man was busy mocking the little girl, the detective harnessed his rage and forced himself to his feet, awkwardly spinning the chair he was bound to into his captor. As the shorter man gasped in shock, Kent propelled him into the wall, then broke the chair over his head. Finally, the little man was silent and crumpled into a heap on the floor.

The arms of the chair still dangled from his arms, but Kent didn't trust himself to waste time. Whatever they had given him wasn't finished wreaking its havoc, and he knew it would get the better of him sooner rather than later. He needed to get them both far away before that happened. After all this time, he knew nobody was coming to save him. His men had set him up and probably made sure nobody knew he was alive. If only he hadn't gotten that promotion, this never would have happened...

It was only a few steps to the little girl, but it was a herculean effort to reach her. What would happen at shift change? They would be missed. The guards would lock them back up, and he didn't have the presence of mind to fight them off. Why had he been locked up with only one guard? Where were all the other prisoners? It didn't make sense. None of it made sense. But he wasn't strong enough to be of any use in a prison break. If he could send help for everyone else, he would. He couldn't help anyone except the girl now. That would have to be enough. He could figure out how to live with himself later.

He quickly picked up the frail child and stumbled toward freedom. They must be in a guard shack. Why hadn't he noticed it before? This must be twice the size of the other buildings. He had been studying the area, looking for an escape, and thought he had memorized the layout. This new building would make it harder to find his way out, but he wasn't giving up now. Not when he was so close.

The farther he walked, the weaker he felt. His aching legs felt like lead; the world was spinning faster with each step and his head getting lighter. It was almost impossible to tell if he was standing straight anymore, but he had to keep going. Suddenly he realized wasn't walking anymore; he was falling, and there was nothing he could do to stop it. All he could do was shelter his precious cargo to keep her safe on the way down.

With a loud thud, he hit the floor. He tried to get up again, then he tried to crawl. It was no use; he couldn't move. As gently as he could, he released the little girl. "G-go..."

Once again, he felt himself slipping away. As everything dissolved into black, he attempted to push her away. The last thing he felt was her little hand rubbing his face.

Chapter Eleven
The Sorry Cad

As soon as he had disappeared into the brush, Jimmy had discovered a car. Next to it was a man with binoculars, watching the flashing headlights and mouthing something to himself. Jimmy snuck around to the back of the car and slid into the back seat, remaining silent as they drove away.

The car stopped. After several minutes, the man stepped out and spit, then glanced at his watch. "Boss said to wait ten minutes before shutting the door. That should be...now."

He slammed the door and started toward the house. This was somewhere new, so Jimmy studied it. The yard was overgrown, but the growth seemed like the result of weeks, not years. Even the house looked like it had gotten a makeover; at first glance, it was old and neglected, but a closer look in the morning sun showed otherwise. The vines on the porch weren't attached to anything; they had been pulled up and staged. Little shards of glass glinted in the sun, revealing that the windows had been broken from the inside.

This was obviously a setup, and probably intended for Kent. Jimmy slipped out of the back seat, but his crutch caught on a stone. "Begorrah," he muttered, hoping the man hadn't heard.

He had. Whoever this man was, he spun to face Jimmy, pistol in hand. Jimmy dove to the ground with the other man right behind him, and the two began a vicious exchange of punches. Even though Jimmy was the better fighter, the man had positioned himself where the blinding sun was behind him, forcing Jimmy to squint his eyes and look into the sun if he was going to see his attacker.

Closing his eyes, he listened. It cost him several kicks as he adjusted to moving by sound, including one that landed in his ear and made his jaw ache, but he finally caught on. When his attacker stepped on a stick, Jimmy pinpointed where the next blow would come from. Hearing the air whoosh, Jimmy braced, then caught the man's leg and twisted.

With the goon sprawled out, Jimmy repositioned himself. The sun was behind him now, his foe lying flat on the ground; he lunged at the man. Time to end the fight. Kent could be in trouble, and here he was, stuck outside.

The thought distracted him. The thug took advantage and wrapped his legs around Jimmy's neck and squeezed. He couldn't reach his crutches yet, but he needed to do something.

Struggling to free himself, he landed a punch to the thug's kidney. Everything was going black and his face felt like it would explode if he didn't get air. The kidney punch had caused the man to grunt, but his grip hadn't relaxed.

Jimmy knew he only had a few moments before it was all over, and his hand desperately clawed at the ground until his fingers closed on a rock. He slammed it into the man's knee and could finally take a breath. Wheezing and gagging, there wasn't time to relax. His foe was already bracing for another attack, but the pain blinded him.

As the thug lunged at Jimmy again, the detective swung the rock, connecting with the man's head. The fight was over, but the man had one last surprise for Jimmy. The momentum was enough to knock the detective backward into the car, and he saw stars.

††††††††††††††††††††††††††

JIMMY BLINKED AT THE bright light in his eyes, his breathing labored. It took him a moment to realize there was a weight on his chest, and he quickly began exploring it with his hands. Just because his eyes wouldn't let him see yet didn't mean he was blind.

There was a person on him; probably an enemy. It was always better to be safe than sorry, so he struggled until he had tied the man up. A few more minutes to get himself together couldn't hurt, so he leaned back against the car.

††††††††††††††††††††††††

HE DIDN'T KNOW HOW long it had been, but at least two hours had passed since Jimmy had closed his eyes. What had been a moment's rest had morphed into an unconscious blur, and he wasn't willing to waste any more time. Now that his prisoner was safely stashed in the trunk, Jimmy retrieved his crutches and moved inside. He heard somebody mumbling and followed the sounds around the corner, his pistol ready.

"Boss?"

Kent blinked. The voice was so familiar—could it be? "Seargent?"

Jimmy looked at Kent, fear and worry etched on his face. Something was very, very wrong, if Kent was calling him that. Still, he needed to make certain that there was nobody else waiting to kill them before he could find out what was ailing his friend. Kent and little

Suki were both breathing, so he had some time. In the next room, he found the realtor, Jack Logan, shaking his head and trying to sit up.

When he saw Jimmy, Logan growled and reached for his pistol.

If he meant to be menacing, he failed. "Right then, ye sorry cad. Ye asked for it."

Jimmy brought the heavy support from his crutch down on the man's head, and he fell to the ground again. "Hard way works for me just fine, after what ye did to me friend."

He pulled the man's arm through the crutch and cuffed him, then began working back toward the car, pausing when he reached Kent's side. "I'll be back quick as a flash, Boss. Wait on me."

With that, he left Kent lying on the floor, still trying to piece together what was happening. He didn't want to get his sergeant captured, and he couldn't stand the thought of the little girl being held in such inhumane conditions. If he didn't get away, he'd fail them both, but his body refused to listen to him. All he could do was keep trying to send her away.

He was still trying to tell her to leave when he heard footsteps. Somebody was coming, and he was out of time. Listening intently, he tried to push her away.

"Run. Don't—stay. Go."

She wouldn't leave him, so he finally pulled her underneath him. If they were going to get recaptured, he could at least keep her safe from the beating that was coming.

"Boss, it's me. You're safe now, me boyo."

Kent stared vacantly at his friend. This had to be a trick—O'Sullivan would never break rank like that.

"Lieutenant? Lou?"

That was more like it. Could this really be his friend?

Although he tried to keep the little girl hidden, he was too weak and confused. He felt the child being pried from his grasp even as the voice was trying to reassure them both.

"Now, bean chile, how would ye like a ride on a horsey? Just hold tight—not so tight, little lass, even we horses must breathe, ye know!—and do not ye be letting go. Sure and now I only have to get our friend up. Come now, Lou, ye are plenty strong enough to help. Ye cannot expect me to carry ye and this little sprite, not a big man like ye. 'Tis almost done, just lean on me a little longer."

His confused friend was not much help, but Jimmy managed to get them both to his car and drove to the hospital as fast as he dared. With a relieved sigh, he noted Detective Johnstone's car was still in the lot.

When Jimmy blared his horn, Johnstone came running out along with the orderlies. Little Suki clung to Kent, who fought them all with what little strength he had left.

He couldn't hear Jimmy calling to him, trying to talk him down. Men with uniforms were trying to separate him from the child he had sworn to protect. There was no way he was going to let them drag her off to torture and experiment on. He struggled harder; a yelp confirmed he had made contact. If he could only hang on until O'Sullivan or Mac came back with help. Surely they would be back soon; he just had to hold on a little longer.

"Please, Lieutenant. 'Tis only the aid man. Just let him help ye, Lou. Please."

As Kent fought for his life, a nurse came running with a sedative. The last thing Kent heard was the sobs of the little girl, still clinging to him as tightly as her frail little body could.

††††††††††††††††††††††††††

TIME BLURRED TOGETHER. NOT much of it made sense to Kent, but his friends stayed with him as he desperately tried to find his way back to the present. The one constant through all the confusion was the tiny hand clutching his; no matter who else came and left, where his mind took him, there she was. He could sometimes hear O'Sullivan talking to him. Other times, his wife Peg was trying to sweet talk him back. Sometimes Mac was standing watch, while sometimes there was a voice he couldn't place calling out to him. Gradually he realized he was in a hospital; although he wanted to wake up more than anything, something kept dragging him back.

†††††††††††††††††††††††††

KENT BLINKED IN THE warm light of the sun. A loud snore startled him, followed by a quieter one. Slowly, he realized his mind wasn't playing tricks on him; something was on his chest.

Gradually, his mind cleared more. The weight was a person. No, two people. Lauren was sleeping in a chair next to the bed, her arm wrapped firmly around his, head slouched back, and mouth open. Suki was curled up in a tight ball on top of him, and for such a little girl, she had a very big snore.

"Lou?"

Kent blinked as he tried to focus. There he was—Jimmy, looking nervously at his friend, shifting his weight from one crutch to the other.

"Jimmy..."

Jimmy's face erupted in a huge smile. "Boss!"

Both of Kent's sleeping companions jumped, leaving him looking sheepishly at them. "Jimmy, ya didn't have to wake them up."

"William! Well, you and I will need to talk later. For now, I am just so thankful you are back!"

Kent looked at Jimmy, then Lauren, then back at Jimmy.

"'Tis been a long week, Boss. Sure and 'twas beginning to look like we had lost ye again, for good this time. Ye owe an explanation to Campbell, by the way. It has been hard keeping him out, but we figured ye could explain this little escapade."

Kent sighed in exasperation. "Week? I lose more time than I keep lately."

Suddenly, he remembered what had happened the last time he had lost so much time. He had not just been thinking about the worst period of his life; he had been living it. Which meant he had told everybody within hearing about his past. It had improved his relationship with Doris more than anything else in their decade together, but it still embarrassed him to know that she knew his secrets. Often he wondered how much of their new and improved relationship was borne out of her pity for him. What if he had done it again with Lauren?

Is that why they needed to talk? He could only hope she had missed anything embarrassing.

Noticing Suki still clinging silently to his arm, Kent patted her head. "How ya doin', kid?"

Suki buried her head in his chest but kept silent, and Jimmy winked at her before answering Kent. "She has not said a word since I found ye—must be the strong, silent type. The doctors said she was drugged while the blaggards had her, but that be about all they could say for sure. They could not get her off of ye, and it seemed to be doing your sorry self good as well."

Kent patted her head again. "What do ya say? Wanna go see your dad?"

"Boss, ye should take it slow. Ye have been pushed too far, and if I be saying that, ye know it be bad."

Even as he said it, Jimmy knew he had wasted his breath. Kent was slowly standing, and Suki noiselessly slid to his ankle.

That was too much for him, and he fell backward toward the bed. Lauren grabbed him to stop him from falling, and Jimmy balanced next to the little girl.

"Wanna ride, páiste?"

Suki clung to Kent's leg, looking up at him for advice. With a lopsided grin, he nodded, sending her scurrying up Jimmy's arm and onto his back. "Not too tight, little one."

Kent was surprised by how short the walk was. Jimmy walked to the other side of the room and pulled aside the curtain, revealing Masao lying in his bed. "Here, little chile. Your da needs his little priss."

He gently leaned over to let her down onto the bed, but she immediately reached for Kent. Though he had only made it to the middle of the room, he still mustered a weak smile for her. "I'll be right there. Good thing you grabbed the hot rod, huh? This slowpoke just got passed by a snail."

She giggled for a moment, but kept reaching for him. He waved to her, but couldn't speed up, so he took advantage of the walk to ask Lauren some questions without his little audience. Hoping to keep the little girl from overhearing, he spoke in a whisper. "Why ain't he awake yet? He was shaken up the last time I seen him, but he was talking."

Lauren whispered back what little she knew. Sometime after Kent had been arrested, two men had arrived and left with the Nagasakis, and they hadn't wasted any time before they started torturing him. After everything else he had been through, it was too much for him. His captors had left him for dead and dumped him out of the car. Although Lauren was only seconds behind them, he hadn't woken up since.

"He probably doesn't have anything left to fight for," Kent muttered sympathetically, prompting his temporary crutch to look at him curiously. The last two years had been intense, and she thought she knew all his secrets, yet he obviously had more to tell. The last week had left her with so many questions, and Jimmy steadfastly refused to answer each. Although she knew now wasn't the time to ask, her inquisitive stare let him know that, sooner rather than later, he was going to have some tough questions to face.

He finally made it to Masao, collapsing instantly into the chair Jimmy had readied for him, then noticed his friend's mischievous expression. "What?"

"Oh, 'tis nothing, me boyo. I was just thinking, this be like old times."

"How do you figure that?"

"'Til ye got me all busted up, I was always faster than ye, and saving ye from trouble besides. 'Tis good to be the nimble one again, even if it only be because ye are in a bad way."

"Ha! Your memory's dotty, old man. You got saved first, and it took me only a few days to find ya. And you were never faster than me—well, except for your temper. You were practically retirement age by the time

I came along. If the army wasn't so hard up for men, you'd a been shipped back."

"I was barely ten years older than ye, and 'twas all wisdom, not age. Ye got captured to save me, and I knew I could do better than that."

Kent chuckled. "Agree to disagree, old timer, but don't ever think you were faster. I ran circles around you so bad you had to get crutches just to steady yourself when I blew past you."

The two bantered a little longer, then Jimmy left for home and a very impatient wife, leaving Lauren free to interrogate her friend. Kent waited nervously, but the questions never came, and he finally realized she wanted him completely isolated before the attack. Now he was doubly thankful for his little shadow, and crossed his fingers that Lauren would forget her questions before Suki's attention shifted back to her father.

†††††††††††††††††††††††††

Kent had several hours of rest before his next visitor arrived. Sloane walked in; his face still bruised but slowly healing. "Irish left word that you were back among the living. You feel up to identifying somebody?"

Suki darted from her father to Kent, who squeezed her little hand. "Only if my pal here can come."

Sloane agreed and swiped a wheelchair, ignoring Kent's protests and pausing for a giggling Lauren to take a photo before rolling him to the car. Although she wanted to come with him, Kent convinced her to keep Masao company until he came back.

The two rode in silence for a few minutes before Kent's curiosity got the better of him. "You're still a pretty decent flat foot,"

"Gee, thanks,"

"And, from what I've seen, you've been extra careful since that goliath almost punched your ticket."

"Is there a point in here somewhere? Or is this payback for the roll of shame?"

"Shame? I got you to do my walking for me. Unlike you, I get plenty of exercise with my job. Point is, how'd a fat oaf like that weaselly captain get the drop on you? There musta been a reason."

Sloane cleared his throat, then purposefully avoided looking at Kent. "There is, and I'd rather it not get around, Lieutenant."

"Yeah, you keep that lieutenant bit quiet and we've got no problem. I'll expect you to fill me in on anything embarrassing I said later, though."

Kent's attempt to ease the sudden tension fell flat. Sloane still gripped the steering wheel as though his life depended on it, despite doing his best to look calm. "Well, Tim and I go way back."

"Like you went to school together?"

"Like he's my older brother. Dad walked out on Mom and I when I was two, but he took Tim with him. Mom had a tough time, but we did all right. Once I turned ten, the old man started getting me for a couple weeks here and there, and all I wanted was to follow my big brother around.

"He was seventeen then, and you can imagine how thrilled he was about having a goofy kid copying his every move. Reckon he was a bully even then, but after the old man got killed on the job, he got worse. He even took the old man's job, but that just made the two of them more alike than ever. Guess I just thought my big brother was still in there somewhere. Well, I kept a list of everything he ever covered up, and I've been working on building a case against him. With that last mistake he made, I've got enough evidence to make him pay for everything."

Kent nodded, not wanting to pry any further, but making a mental note to find everything he could to keep the former captain behind bars for the rest of his life. If he hated the man before, he loathed him now.

The rest of the drive was short and silent. Kent had

never been so thankful to get out of a car in his life, even if he had to put up with some snickers as Sloane wheeled him through the room. Only a few dared to laugh, and a stern glare from the policeman shut them all up.

Kent wasn't content to just identify the man. He wanted to ensure the crook paid for his crime without Suki being forced to testify.

A confession would do that nicely, but Jimmy's thug was stubborn and listened to his lawyer. The evidence against him was circumstantial. Jail wasn't fun, but he was certain it was temporary.

Although Suki didn't want to let Kent leave, he convinced her she could watch from behind a screen. He knew the little girl would be safe as long as she was out of sight.

Leaving the wheelchair in the hall, Kent steadied himself before walking into the room, smirking with satisfaction when the man paled.

"You ok, fella? You look positively green."

"I thought—well, I heard..."

"I ain't dead yet, no matter what ya thought." Kent turned the chair backward before straddling it. "And what's more, neither is Masao Nagasaki."

Kent noted with pleasure that the man looked more

worried than ever. "So, you thought he was circling the drain, too? Well, you've got to get better sources, fella. Your info is as rotten as you are. He kept notes on all his friends that your boss rubbed out, and now I've got it."

"Why didn't you use it before?"

"You might not've noticed, but even though he hired me, he was from the losing side of history. That, plus how y'all terrorized his community, made him suspicious. He almost took it to his grave, but lucky for the good guys, he's actually a pretty tough character."

"I already said I'm not talking."

Kent stood up, pulling himself to his full height before sitting on the table next to the thoroughly terrified man. He leaned close to the man's ear and whispered, not wanting anyone else to hear what was said. "I don't want you to talk. You and your boss—I want you to walk. It takes a special kind of evil to do what you did to that little girl. When this goes to trial, I'm gonna lie. I'm gonna make sure you walk free, then I'm gonna take you both. I'm gonna feed you the same stuff you gave Suki, and I'm gonna watch you drool your way to the grave."

"You can't do that!"

Kent smirked. "Look, I can't do it. You're right. I've been working this a long time, and I know how to take you while a dozen people swear I've been with them. I don't like killing—takes a little piece of you every time you do it.

"In your case, though, I bet it'll do the opposite. Erasing trash like you from the face of the earth oughta give me some of my soul back. Knowing scum like you are walking around, that you might hurt her one day? <u>That</u> would kill me. I will be there to watch you every minute until you take your last breath. And believe me, starvation is a rough way to go. I lost a lot of friends to it, and still have its scars. You were willing to do that to a little girl; gave her just enough food to keep her drugged. I cannot wait to see how you look when it's happening to you."

Shaking with fear, the man pushed himself as far away from Kent as possible. The cold, calculating stare let him know how serious the detective was, and he didn't plan on giving Kent a chance to follow through with his threats. "Hey out there—I'll say anything you want. I want to tell you absolutely everything."

"You're no fun." Kent stood and walked out before collapsing into the chair, while little Suki quickly scurried out of her hiding spot and back into his lap.

Glancing at Sloane, Kent shrugged. "What? I just put some of the fear of God in him. Had a little talk, and now he's ready to spill his guts. Sounds like a win to me."

The goon was true to his word. Over the next few hours, he told everything; how the neighborhood was about to become an interstate, and the land value would skyrocket. Logan had an insider, and all he had to do to become rich was get control of the land. He had hired the delinquents to do that, coming up with the idea of framing the Klan just in case somebody got interested.

Until Nagasaki, it had worked like a charm. He had outsmarted them when they came. In him, it looked like they had met their match.

From out of nowhere, Misa Nagasaki had tracked them down. She wanted to sell and was willing to do whatever it took to get back to her home in Japan. She told them everything they needed to know to get the drop on her husband.

Although she didn't want her husband hurt at first, she changed her mind as soon as she learned he was getting outside help. She had set up that first beating, then decided to kill Kent on her own. The delinquents had been sent to deal with him, not knowing he had already been poisoned.

When they left, he was ordered to eliminate the young hooligans and frame Kent for their murder. The detective himself was supposed to die in the fire;

when he didn't, they had been forced to change their plans and went to his neighbor for help. She had been too happy to get rid of him, but she had too much information about them. As soon as her statement was on the record, they had silenced her and framed Kent for that, too.

When Lauren overheard Logan and Misa talking, they decided to shut her up, too, so they set a trap for her in the swamp. He didn't know what happened to the man hired to kill her, but Misa had called to give them a location after knocking Masao out. They were supposed to dispose of Lauren, but they hadn't been able to find her.

When Masao had woken up in the car, he was angry and hurt, but still refused to sign anything until he knew his children were safe. The thug admitted it had been his job to beat the man into submission, but Masao had collapsed instead. Since he wasn't breathing, they dumped his body so it would be identified. Then Misa would inherit the property and sign it over to them.

When Masao's name didn't appear in the obituaries, they asked around and discovered he wasn't dead. The boss decided to kill Misa, finish Masao off while he was still hospitalized, and buy their land at a public sale.

Instead, Misa had been saved, and Masao was under guard.

At this point, Logan wanted nothing more than revenge. He decided to lure Kent to the house where Suki was being held and hid a needle in the doorknob. The headlights were a signal; the thug was supposed to drive around for thirty minutes, then park the car nearby, wait another ten minutes, and slam the door. After that, he was expected to go inside and help move Kent, who would be unconscious, into the room for his torture, and then come back later to help take his body and dump it at Masao's as a warning to Mrs. Watanabe. Instead, Jimmy had surprised him, leading to the current conversation.

"Well, we'll see about getting you bail, but I can't promise anything," Sloane said. "After all, you were party to a lot of murders, even if you didn't commit them all yourself."

"No! I did it. I deserve to pay. I'll testify against Logan, but just lock me up so I can do my time. Whatever the judge says, I'm ready for it...I'm ashamed of what I did."

Sloane arched an eyebrow and stared suspiciously at the door, but Kent was very pleased with himself. The thug had just confessed to nine murders. He would probably never get out. And since Logan had paid for or committed nearly twenty murders and one kidnapping, never mind all the attempted murder charges, he shouldn't either.

†††††††††††††††††††††††††

IT HAD BEEN TWO weeks since Kent had woken up, and the hardest thing he had faced was telling Campbell what had happened. The Aussie had taken it badly, but Suki had quickly won him over. He had even started sneaking her little gifts when he got off work, and she had rewarded him with several smiles in return.

Thanks to Suki, Kent had successfully avoided being alone with Lauren. The little girl was gradually relaxing, but still refused to be in a different room from her hero. Still, he knew it was only a matter of time.

Lauren had finally cornered him in the kitchen when he was making Suki a sandwich. "Look, William, I want you to understand that I do not expect to know everything about your past. If you are not comfortable telling me about being a soldier, that's quite reasonable. My father never wanted to speak about it either. However, I do expect to hear about women who still hold your affection."

"Well, there's this aggravating kid who's kind of grown on me—you know, like a wart?"

"As flattering as that is, I'm interested in 'Peg'. When

you were so—ill—it wasn't my name you called, and I want to know why. I'm curious to know why it took you nearly dying for me to find out about her."

"Because she's my past, Lars. I got a Dear John from her the day I was captured and never saw her again."

"So, why did you call her name?"

"Let me ask you somethin'. What year was it, for me, I mean?"

"Jimmy said 1945..."

"How old were you then? Eight? Even if I had met you, that'd be weird, and it's even stranger to be carryin' on about a kid I'd never met."

"But you have met me, and wanted to go out with me, but when you really needed me, you forgot I existed."

"And believe me, nobody hates that more than I do. You are my Bacall, and if I'm dyin', I'd much rather be thinkin' about you than her. I'da had a much better time if I wasn't rememberin' her. I married Peg when I was seventeen, could never make enough to afford the things she liked, and barely six months later Pearl Harbor got bombed. I shipped out the next day and never saw her again. She got the marriage annulled, and it was Mac and Jimmy what got me through the next few years.

"When I first met you, you were worried about being

labeled crazy. I don't blame you. They locked me up for it, and from what I can remember, I wouldn't recommend it to anyone. Mac asked her to come see me through it, but she refused. She was the love of my life then, and she was all I wanted. Then. I do not now or ever want to see her again. I don't care about her one way or another, although until I met you, I hated her guts. If she hadn't dumped me, I wouldn't have met you, and she'd have probably worked me to death by now—or taken out an insurance policy and gotten me whacked to collect the money.

"If you ever tell anybody any of this, I'll never talk to you again, but I reckon you should know before—well, I mean, if we're goin' steady. And if I really called you her name, take it as a compliment—I might not've known it was you, but I still knew you were my love. Just had to give you the name I knew then to make it all fit and not go completely bonkers."

It was a lot to process, but Lauren felt bad for her friend. Even though she wanted to understand everything, she still knew little more than when she had walked in, but what she had learned was enough for now. Maybe, one day, he would explain the rest, but at least she knew who Kent had been dreaming about. He was the same person she had always known, not some philanderer with a wife she knew nothing about. He was still hers.

She wrapped her arms around his waist before showing him out of the kitchen. "I've seen what you can make. I'll fix lunch. Maybe after we eat, we can take Suki to visit her father."

†††††††††††††††††††††††††

Masao was still unconscious when they got to the hospital, but Suki was getting used to that. She wasn't scared of him anymore, and clambered up to perch next to him on the bed. The little girl hadn't spoken since her rescue, but she had been having a good day. She had exciting news, and she was tired of him sleeping through her visits.

"Otōsan! Up, sleepyhead. I got new toy, and my fwend show me how to shoot."

Kent grimaced. "Great. You finally decide to talk, and then you go and say that."

Masao moaned but still didn't wake up, and Kent exhaled in relief. "Missy, it's good to hear you and all that, but next time, try not to say something that'll make him wanna kill me, okay?"

Kent called Mrs. Watanabe, who had been watching the boys since they had been retrieved from the hotel where Misa had left them. They steadfastly refused to visit and had only been to the hospital once. Even then, she had forced them to come; they blamed him for everything that had happened, just like their mother had. After all, she had been the one explaining everything to them. Misa had successfully convinced them it was all their father's fault. She was still wreaking havoc on her family, even after being safely locked away.

Chapter Twelve
The Midnight Shift

Kent felt sorry for Masao, but he had a new worry—one that he had never had before.

"Her first day of school is tomorrow. She's out of time off. What do I do?" Kent whispered to Lauren.

"I'd ask Jimmy. She is nearly James Junior's age, and they are probably in the same class. Maybe Mrs. O'Sullivan can help get her to the right place. We can take her shopping this afternoon for whatever supplies she might need."

Suki had already befriended both O'Sullivan children, and Doris had just finished making the little girl some new dresses for school. She agreed to bring the two over to spend the night with the girl and take her to school in the morning, with Kent standing by in case she retreated into her shell again.

As soon as Suki went to bed, Kent returned to the

hospital to keep Masao company, just like every other night. He was only a phone call away if she woke up, but he didn't want Masao to find himself alone when he finally regained consciousness; Kent knew firsthand how hard it was to fight when there was nothing left to fight for. So he spent the midnight shift describing what Suki had done all day.

Tonight would probably be the same as every other night. Suki had left her favorite stuffed bear with her father, and as always, Kent put it next to Masao's cheek so he could smell her. His own strength was almost back, but that didn't mean he planned to spend the night pacing; he sat in a chair and got comfortable before beginning his nightly one-sided conversation.

He was still rambling about a painting Suki had made when a weak voice interrupted him. "What-what she shoot?"

Kent was almost as surprised as he had been when Suki had spoken earlier that day, but was determined not to startle his companion. "My buddy wanted her to be able to defend herself if anybody ever came at her again, so she can use a slingshot and a boomerang now. Sorry about that, I know you shoulda been the one to teach her, if you even wanted her to know. In his defense, I asked your permission a week ago, and you didn't answer. I figured if anything was gonna snap you outta that funk, it would be that question, but it didn't. Honestly, I feel better knowing she can defend herself, too. When she starts school tomorrow, Jimmy's kids will look after her. They both know how to take care of themselves, but now she doesn't have to rely on that. She can look after herself."

Masao opened his eyes for a moment before tiredly closing them again. By now, the nurse was examining him, and Kent waited patiently for her to finish.

By the time she was done, Masao was completely alert and insisting on finding out what had happened. Not wanting to compromise the case, Kent steadfastly refused to say anything other than that it was over, Suki was safe, and a police detective was coming to take his statement.

Sloane showed up thirty minutes later, his pajamas peeking out from under his coat; a cup of coffee in one hand, notepad in the other. There wasn't much Masao could add that they hadn't figured out, especially since he had large chunks of his memory missing, but he vividly remembered Misa's treachery.

"When you take Detective-san away, I was most careless. I go to window to see where he was going, even though he warned me about her. I should have listened to most honorable detective, but to my unending shame, I did not. She surprised me. I turned in time to see her, but not avoid her. She put a cloth on my face, and to my eternal disgrace, she was stronger than I.

"The next time that I know anything, we were in a car. She tell me sign papers, and we would get Suki back, but I know they will kill her if they do not need her anymore. So I refuse. They try to beat me, but I not so weak as to sacrifice my little girl for that. Then I could not breathe, they say I dead, and my wife says to throw me out. Your young friend was suddenly there, but I remember little after, except that my daughter is now safe."

Seeing how tired and weak the man was, Sloane left soon after, allowing Masao to collapse back onto his pillow, exhausted. Too weak to open his eyes, he could only mumble his thanks. "Please accept my thanks, Detective-san. You have my undying gratitude for all you have done for my family."

Kent shuffled awkwardly. "Only thing I did was drop a bomb on your family."

"It was not you that did that, but my wife. You saved my daughter at great personal cost. You are very honorable, Detective-san."

"I almost let them finish you off that first day."

"And I am surprised you did not. Were the tables

turned, I would have."

"Yeah, somehow I ain't buying that. Pretty sure you'd a done the same I did."

"At any rate, you take care of my family when I could not. Thank you for protecting my Suki. I have only one request of you now. If it is not too much trouble, could I see her after school?"

Kent agreed, finished explaining everything to Masao, and started to leave. Before he could, the phone rang. The call was unexpected enough before he heard Sloane's voice, but his friend's words caught him completely off guard.

Sloane had gone to work, planning to type up the final addition to his report; his friends had a report for him instead. Sometime over the past four hours, both Misa Nagasaki and Jack Logan had committed suicide, while the two thugs had been killed trying to escape.

Kent was immediately suspicious. He knew the man Jimmy had captured was terrified of him, and wouldn't have tried to escape. He was confident of that. But he couldn't exactly tell Sloane about the threats he had made, so his efforts to convince his friend that the deaths were suspicious fell on deaf ears. Sloane insisted that, given the charges they were facing, none of it was surprising.

After the phone call disconnected, Kent told Masao it was over for good. <u>Everyone</u> involved was dead. Masao understood, but his face remained expressionless, aside from a deep sadness in his eyes.

†††††††††††††††††††††††††

"Too bad Misa Nagasaki couldn't have seen this—she'd have never wanted to go anywhere close to a bomb site." Kent joked as his young date jumped and hid her face in his jacket. He laughed at her, and she felt defensive.

"Well, this *could* happen. All this technology is very new, you know," Lauren defended herself, suddenly flinching as gunfire erupted from the speaker on the window.

The movie was several months old, but Lauren hadn't seen it yet. There was something about being at a drive-in that made every movie an immersive experience, and this was no exception.

For her, anyway. Kent wasn't buying any of it. "Yeah, and the radioactive gook might make everybody grow a working brain. This is the funniest thing I've ever seen, Graves or not."

Lauren wasn't giving up. "We don't know what the materials could do. In the long run, it could cause any number of mutations. It could do anything,"

"Anything except make a good movie."

"William, hush."

As the giant bugs disappeared from the screen, Kent yelled and jumped at her, causing her to shriek. "William Kent, you are despicable!"

"So they say, but you know that's why you love me."

"Hmph! More like why I feel sorry for you."

As they pulled out of the parking lot, Kent switched his lights on. "Well, that was fun, anyway, no matter how hokey it was. Work's been slow lately, so at least this was somethin'. Reckon I've cracked all the tough cases I'll get, now that I've faced my fears and all that jazz."

Kent needn't have worried. Despite his fear of being stuck working only straightforward jobs for the rest of his life, Lauren knew that trouble was only ever one case away. Soon, Kent took a job as dangerous as it was confusing; 'The Counterfeit Grave' was destined to be his most baffling case yet.

But that was the future. Now it was after midnight, and Kent was headed to the diner, hoping Campbell would cook a double cheeseburger with extra fries.

THE END

A Word to the Reader

Thank you for reading! The fifth book in this series, *The Counterfeit Grave*, will be published on November 5th, 2024.

If you enjoyed this book, please leave a review on amazon.com, Goodreads, or any of your favorite book hangouts.

Be the first to know about exclusive content, new releases, cover reveals and more by following on Instagram, facebook.com/RPHollis, or joining the Facebook group *The Kent Detective Agency*.

Slang from The Rose of Death
In Order of Use

Masao

(Japanese)

Hai—Yes

-San—Friend (Someone younger than you)

Tsuma—Wife

Dōmo arigatōgozaimashita—Thank you very much

Onna—Woman

Chad

(Australian slang)

Maggot—A reprehensible or despicable person

Stickybeak—A busybody; meddler

Kent

(Southern slang, historical events)

In for a penny, in for a pound—used to say that a person should finish what he or she has started to do even though it may be difficult or expensive

Hell ships—Allied prisoners of war called them "hell ships," the requisitioned merchant vessels that the Japanese navy overloaded with POWs being relocated to internment on the Japanese Home Islands or elsewhere in the empire. The holds were floating dungeons, where inmates were denied air, space, light, bathroom facilities, and adequate food and water—especially water. Thirst and heat claimed many lives in the end, as did summary executions and beatings, yet the vast majority of deaths came as a result of so-called "friendly fire" from U.S. and Allied naval ships, submarines, and aircraft

Tommy Atkins—Slang for a common soldier in the British Army Trivia—Judy Garland sang a song called 'Chin Up! Cheerio! Carry On! (Don't Give Up Tommy Atkins)' in Babes on Broadway https://www.youtube.com/watch?v=I8g3dSL5xu8

Blitz—A series of bombing raids by the German Air Force (Luftwaffe) on British cities and towns during World War II, from September 1940 to May 1941

Twisting in the wind—Left in a very difficult and weak position, often by people who hope to gain advantage from this for themselves

Behind the eight-ball—In a difficult situation or tight

spot; at a disadvantage

Drop you—Knock you out, punch you

Aces—Of both people and objects, wonderful, marvelous, excellent

Gaga—Infatuated

Jimmy

(Irish)

Mo ghrá—My love

Cailín—Girl

Da—Dad

Black and Tans—Due to the heightening tension between British colonial forces and Irish nationals, the police forces were augmented with military veterans from World War I who became known as the Black and Tans. The Black and Tans were more brutal than ordinary police officers. The majority of them were British, which meant they had less sympathy for the Irish cause, and their military training made them more able to reciprocate violence.

Easter Rising—On Easter Monday 1916, Irish nationalists launched an armed revolt against British rule in Ireland. Although quickly suppressed by the British Army, the rising was a seminal moment in modern Irish history, helping pave the way to the nation's independence in 1922.

Floozy—A young woman who has many casual sexual partners; one who dresses or behaves in a sexually provocative way.

Leannán—Lover

Mo chroí—My heart

Garsún—Boy

Deartháir—Brother

Oubliette—A forgetting place, like a dungeon: Example: Leap Castle has a famous Oubliette

Banshee—a female spirit in Gaelic folklore whose appearance or wailing warns a family that one of them will soon die

Shattered—Exhausted

Beagnach maraíodh—Almost killed

Picked a comb up—In Irish folklore, some people believe that you should never pick up a comb found on the ground because it may belong to a banshee. The banshee is a female spirit that is often depicted combing her long silver hair, and picking up her comb may attract her attention. Some say that if you do pick up the comb, the banshee will come to your window that night looking for it back. Others say that if you pick up a comb and bring it home, the banshee will come at night crying for it.

Páiste—Child

Doris

(Gaelic)

Glaikit—Foolish; silly; thoughtless

Nae—Not

Auld mahoun—The Devil

Cladhaires—Coward (Irish)

Mo ghaol—My love

Mo chridhe—My heart

An duine agam—My husband

Murdered Neighbor

(Slang)

Trollop—A woman who has many casual sexual encounters or relationships

Mrs. Watanabe

(Japanese)

Yokai—Apparition

Suki

(Japanese)

Otōsan—Dad

Thanks to Google, Wordhippo, https://modernisms.tripod.com/group/id15.htmlhttps://www.dictionary.com/browse/stickybeakhttps://www.history.navy.mil/browse-by-topic/wars-conflicts-and-operations/world-war-ii/1944/oryoku-maru.htmlhttps://en.wikipedia.org/wiki/Tommy_Atkinshttps://w

ww.collinsdictionary.com/us/dictionary/english/twisting-in-the-wind#:~:text=or%20swinging%20in%20the%20wind,advantage%20from%20this%20for%20themselveshttps://en.wiktionary.org/wiki/behind_the_eight-ball#:~:text=(idiomatic)%20In%20a%20difficult%20situation,really%20behind%20the%20eight%2Dball.https://www.urbandictionary.com/define.php?term=drop%20youhttps://greensdictofslang.com/entry/33wlzzy#:~:text=1.,%3B%20thus%20you're%20aces!https://www.merriam-webster.com/dictionary/gaga#:~:text=informal%20%3A%20marked%20by%20extreme%20enthusiasm,is%20gaga%20about%2Fover%20golf.htt ps://www.irelandwithlocals.com/irish-slang-and-what-they-mean/https://www.collinsdictionary.com/us/dictionary/english/glaikit#:~:text=glaikit%20in%20British%20English,foolish%3B%20silly%3B%20thoughtlesshttps://www.thebottleimp.org.uk/2011/11/scots-word-of-the-season-mahoun/?print=print

https://study.com/academy/lesson/black-tans-overview-history-legacy.html#:~:text=Due%20to%20the%20heightening%20tension,brutal%20than%20ordinary%20police%20officers.https://www.nam.ac.uk/explore/easter-rising#:~:text=On%20Easter%20Monday%201916%2C%20Irish,the%20nation's%20independence%20in%201922. and local dialect

About the Author

R. P. Hollis grew up vacationing around beautifully haunted St. Augustine, Florida, and devouring all the ghost stories she could find. She is an avid mystery reader who loves Nancy Drew mysteries even now that she's grown, married, and has two little children; she finds solace in writing. Although she has been writing since she was ten, The Pirate's Curse is her first published book. She enjoys writing her mysteries and hopes you enjoy reading them as much as she enjoyed writing them! Find her on fb at fb.com/RPHollis

Afterword

What are worthless and wicked people like? They are constant liars, signaling their deceit with a wink of the eye, a nudge of the foot, or the wiggle of fingers. Their perverted hearts plot evil, and they constantly stir up trouble. But they will be destroyed suddenly, broken in an instant beyond all hope of healing. There are six things the Lord hates—no, seven things he detests: haughty eyes, a lying tongue, hands that kill the innocent, a heart that plots evil, feet that race to do wrong, a false witness who pours out lies, a person who sows discord in a family. Proverbs 6:16-19

List of Kent Detective Agency Mysteries

1: The Pirate's Curse (Nov. 1, 2022)
2: The Poison Pen (July 4, 2023)
3: The Fatal Reunion (Nov. 7, 2023)
4: The Rose of Death (July 2, 2024)
5: The Counterfeit Grave (Nov 5, 2024)
6: The Deadly Deception (July 1, 2025)
7: The Final Showdown (Nov. 4, 2025)